A VOTE FOR LOVE

"You know, Donna," Elaine said. "I'd really hate to see you get hurt, so I hope you won't mind my being a little brutal. I've known Tad a long time. Believe me, I'm only saying this now so you won't be upset later."

I put the brushes down on the counter. "What is it, Elaine?"

She sighed. "Well, Tad is what he is. Charming. Fun. But in spite of what he says now, he likes your art, not you. And when the campaign is over, I'm afraid your relationship will be, too."

I could feel tears forming in my eyes. "That's not true," I said defensively. "You don't know anything about Tad and me."

"Oh, Donna." There was an edge of scorn in Elaine's voice. "Don't be so naive."

Bantam Sweet Dreams Romances
Ask your bookseller for the books you have missed

Bantam Sweet Dreams Specials

A Vote For Love

Terri Fields

BANTAM BOOKS

TORONTO • NEW YORK • LONDON • SYDNEY • AUCKLAND

RL 6, IL age 11 and up

A VOTE FOR LOVE
A Bantam Book / July 1988

Sweet Dreams and its associated logo are registered trademarks of
Bantam Books, Inc. Registered in U.S. Patent and Trademark
Office and elsewhere.

Cover photo by Pat Hill.

ISBN 0-553-26672-1

Published simultaneously in the United States and Canada

Bantam Books are published by Bantam Books, Inc. Its trademark,
consisting of the words "Bantam Books" and the portrayal of a
rooster, is Registered in U.S. Patent and Trademark Office and in
other countries. Marca Registrada, Bantam Books, Inc., 666 Fifth
Avenue, New York, New York 10103.

Printed and bound in Great Britain by
Hazell Watson & Viney Limited
Member of BPCC plc
Aylesbury Bucks

With love to Rick, Lori, Jeff
and Janet Fields

· Chapter One

My stomach flip-flopped nervously as I walked into art class. Mrs. Gibbons had promised to return our semester projects that day. We'd already waited almost two weeks to get our grades, and I hoped Mrs. Gibbons wouldn't torture us anymore by not giving the projects back until the end of the period.

Slipping into my seat, I thought of all the hours I'd spent on my oil painting of a bowl and pitcher sitting on a table. There was a window in the background, and the light that streamed through it cast shadows on the table. I'd started the painting over a hundred times, hoping to make it absolutely perfect. Getting a good grade was important if I wanted to get into the Art Institute of America. Mentally I checked off the criteria again. My painting had been original. It had been visually balanced and had also demonstrated good technique and use of color. But was it a painting worthy of an A? I opened my notebook and peeked again at the folded brochure I kept clipped to the inside cover. The flyer looked a little ragged because I'd carried it with me everywhere for months. I'd even underlined one sentence in bright pink felt tip for inspiration: "The Art Institute of America accepts only the country's most promising young artists."

Letting out a heavy sigh, I absently twirled a strand of my long blond hair. Everything had seemed so easy such a short time ago when I'd lived in Yankton, South Dakota. There, I'd been known as the school artist. My teachers had all told me I'd have no problem getting into the Art Institute after high school. But then we had moved to Tucson, Arizona, and I went from being the star to being just one of many students in an advanced art class. Mrs. Gibbons was much more critical of my work than any art teacher I'd ever had before, and I worked extra hard to earn her respect. So far I wasn't doing quite so well as I had hoped, although I had to admit that Mrs. Gibbons was a fair grader. She just *had* to like my painting. I had practically killed myself doing it, and I knew it was one of my best.

Class finally started, and I was relieved when I saw that Mrs. Gibbons was going to hand our projects back right away. "May I have your attention?" she began. "I'm really pleased with your semester art projects, and I'm sorry that it has taken me so long to return them. I wanted to consider each one very carefully." She began passing back the projects after explaining that the project grade would be in the top left-hand corner and the semester grade on the bottom. When she put my painting on my desk, I shut my eyes, too nervous to look at it just then. Finally I allowed myself to peek, and I felt the color drain from my face. I'd gotten a B! How was that possible? I'd never gotten such a low grade in art in my whole life.

Somehow I made it through the rest of the period. All the other kids seemed pleased with their grades. I tried not to look as miserable as I felt and focused my attention on class. As soon as the bell rang, I took a deep breath and tried to keep my legs from shaking as I walked up to speak to Mrs. Gibbons.

In most of my other classes a B would have been OK. But in art, it was the end of absolutely everything. I'd never thought of myself as particularly pretty or popular, but my art ability made me feel special. It was my one real talent, and I was sick at the thought that I might not even be very good at that. Had my well-intentioned teachers back in Yankton been mistaken about my gifts? My stomach fell.

As I waited for the other kids to leave, I tried to figure out what I could say that might make Mrs. Gibbons understand how I felt. Finally the classroom emptied out. Forgetting everything I'd been about to tell her, I awkwardly thrust my semester project in front of my teacher. "I—I was hoping I'd get a better grade on this. I worked so hard."

Mrs. Gibbons put her glasses on and looked carefully at my painting. "Well, Donna, there's no doubt that you're one of my best art students, but on this painting you got the grade I felt you deserved." She gave me an understanding smile. "I'm sorry, but the work lacked the sensitivity and warmth a good painting should have. Frankly, Donna, the coldness in your work has concerned me all semester. That's why I've given you a B for your final grade. I think you need to have more fun with art, to make it come more alive."

"I'll really try, honest," I replied. "But please don't give me a B for the semester. You see, I want to go to the Art Institute of America after I graduate, and they only admit the most promising art students," I said in a small voice. "Mrs. Gibbons," I continued with a little more confidence, "I'll do a whole extra project if you want, but please at least give me a chance to raise my grade. I know I can do it."

"Well, I really don't know," replied Mrs. Gibbons, tapping her pencil on the table. "I don't like to make a policy of changing grades." I couldn't look at her as she spoke. My whole future depended on her words. My hands were shaking as I watched her think about my request. "This obviously means a lot to you, Donna, so why don't you let me think about it for a day? Stop by my desk after school tomorrow, and I'll let you know what I've decided."

That night I excused myself from dinner and went to bed early. Tossing and turning, I first dreamed that Mrs. Gibbons told me she would change my grade and then said she wouldn't.

At school the next day my classes passed by in a blur. I hardly spoke to anyone, except for an occasional hello or to answer a question in class. Finally I was standing at Mrs. Gibbons's desk again, silently crossing my fingers. I promised myself that I wouldn't care how much extra work she gave me if it meant I'd get a chance to bring up my grade.

Mrs. Gibbons looked at me. "Yes, Donna?" she asked. Just as I began to wonder if she'd forgotten why I was there, she gestured toward a seat in the front row. "Sit down, and I'll tell you what I've decided." I took a seat and she continued. "I've done a little checking and quite a bit of soul-searching. I'd hate to deny any of my students the chance to attend America's finest art institute. I'm not sure, however"—she smiled slightly—"that one B could affect your application all that much. You do have a great deal of talent. However, I sincerely doubt that you would do well at the Art Institute unless you learn to loosen up a bit and make your paintings warmer and more human."

So many butterflies were dancing in my stomach that I had to fight the urge to shout at Mrs. Gibbons to just tell me what her decision was and not keep me in suspense any longer. Freezing a smile on my face, I forced myself to be patient. I was so nervous that I had difficulty focusing on the rest of her speech.

"I'd like you to do a project for me that will broaden your abilities and add a bit more life to your work," Mrs. Gibbons continued. "And here's what I have in mind. Student government is very important here at Washington High, and elections for class officers are held twice a year."

"Twice?" I asked in surprise.

"That's right," Mrs. Gibbons said. "The administration decided to institute semester elections so that more students could become involved. In any case, the next election is coming up soon, and two seniors are running for student-body president." She smiled. "It should be quite a race. The campaigns sometime include a good deal of artwork— posters, buttons, banners, and so on. I thought that you might benefit from heading the art committee of one of the candidate's campaigns."

I gulped. *Me, run a whole art campaign?* I wouldn't even know where to begin. I'd never become involved in something like *that* before. How would I be able to work with a bunch of kids I didn't even know? I had trouble enough just trying to talk to them.

Mrs. Gibbons was watching me closely. "And so, Donna, this project will help you and the school as well. It might even be fun. Besides, I'd feel perfectly justified in giving you an A after all that additional effort. I don't give away grades, and this way you'll have earned it. Does that seem fair, Donna?"

"Sure, yes." I stumbled all over my words. "I mean, thanks. I'll be glad to do it. I'll make some terrific posters. And—and I really appreciate your giving me another chance, Mrs. Gibbons." I could feel myself blushing bright red, and I eased my way out of the classroom before I could make an even bigger fool of myself.

In the distance I could see my best friends, Sandy and Ellen, waiting for me by my locker. I really don't know how I would have survived at Washington High if it hadn't been for them. I remembered my first few days at Washington vividly, and how I'd had to eat lunch all alone and walk through the halls without anyone to talk to. I felt almost invisible. If I hadn't met Sandy, I would still have been pretty much alone. The very day that Miss Thompson moved Sandy behind me in English, Sandy had introduced herself and invited me to meet her for lunch in the cafeteria. Ellen was Sandy's best friend, and she was at the table, too. At first, I'd been tongue-tied, even though they were so friendly. But it hadn't seemed to matter. Sandy bubbled on at fifty miles an hour, and I soon felt as if I'd known her and Ellen all my life. I showed them some of my work awhile later, and they were convinced that I was going to become a great artist someday. Their confidence in my talent was flattering, but Sandy was the first to admit that she didn't know anything about real art. I laughed and promised them both an original if I ever got to be famous. Right then that didn't seem to be very likely.

As I approached my locker, Sandy burst out, "Well, what did she say? I've been keeping my fingers crossed all afternoon. Is she going to give you an A?" Sandy asked. I had told them both about my problem the day before.

"Well, yes and no." I took a deep breath and smiled at their puzzled looks. "I guess I'm not making much sense, am I? Mrs. Gibbons gave me a chance to earn it," I replied happily. "All I have to do is another project. I'm going to coordinate all the artwork for one of the student-body presidential candidates. You know—posters, buttons, and that kind of stuff. It shouldn't be all that hard."

Sandy looked at Ellen, and Ellen shook her head. "Hey, you guys, what's wrong? Didn't you hear me?" I asked.

"Yeah, we heard," Ellen answered, running a hand through her short red curls. "Donna, you're so out of it sometimes. I'll bet you don't even know who's running for student-body president."

"Sure I do," I replied quickly, and then I began to laugh. "OK, you know me too well. Who's running?"

"Christy Jenkins and Tad Gordon." Sandy said their names with more than a touch of awe.

"Geez," exclaimed Ellen, "the two most popular kids in the whole senior class! You've got to ask one of *them* to let you run their whole art campaign? That's some project Mrs. Gibbons gave you. Why didn't she just ask you to defy gravity and walk into space? Don't teachers ever realize that the really popular kids are different? I wouldn't even know what to say to Christy or Tad."

I saw Sandy nudge Ellen and give her a dirty look. Ellen began to blush as she tried to remove her foot from her mouth. "Oh, that's not really the way it is, Donna. I mean, don't pay any attention to me. Either one of them would probably be glad to get your help. You're a terrific artist."

"Yeah, thanks," I said, sighing miserably. "I guess you guys are right. Asking Christy or Tad to let me run one of their art campaigns is going to be one of the hardest things I've ever done. But if I don't work for one of them,

I'll get a B from Mrs. Gibbons. And if I get a B, I'll never get into the Art Institute. And if I don't get into the Art Institute, well"—I hesitated—"my whole career will go down the drain." Maybe I was exaggerating a bit, but I just couldn't afford to take a chance. I'd been so confident about becoming an artist, and now it looked as if I were going to be a nobody for the rest of my life.

I spent the weekend thinking about the entire mess. But even as I sat cross-legged on my bed Sunday evening, I still hadn't figured out what to do. Where should I begin? I took out a big drawing pad and began to sketch absently. Ellen and Sandy and I had discussed the situation earlier that afternoon. My friends had been sympathetic, but they couldn't really decide for me. I was going to have to figure this all out by myself.

There was no way I could approach Tad Gordon. Like every other girl in school, I'd definitely noticed him. Everything about the guy was absolutely perfect. Over six feet tall, with dark, wavy hair and piercing blue eyes, his rugged face looked like Tom Selleck's. Of course, Tad didn't know it, but earlier that year I had used him as a model for my Roman gods art project. I worked from his newspaper picture as homecoming king. I'd gotten an A on the project, but no one had guessed that it was Tad Gordon who had inspired my drawing. I sighed, picturing him before me. I just didn't have the nerve to walk up to him and start talking.

That left Christy Jenkins. I wasn't quite sure which cheerleader she was, so I had to look her up in the yearbook. She had been last year's prom princess, the outstanding cheerleader—the list went on and on. Her smiling face seemed to stand out from every page. I wasn't sure I could talk to her any more than I could talk to Tad. After all, Christy was a senior, and she had no idea who I was.

My mom walked into my room as I was studying the yearbook. "What are you doing, honey?" she asked.

It was stupid, I know, but I pushed the yearbook toward her. "Mom, do you think this girl looks nice?"

My mother looked at Christy's picture. "Actually, I think you and she look a lot alike."

"Mom!" I said in horror. "That's *Christy Jenkins.* She's head cheerleader and everything."

"Well, that's very nice, dear, but I still think the two of you look alike. Is she a friend of yours? I've never heard you mention her name."

Sooner or later my mom would find out I wasn't doing so well in art, so I took a deep breath and tried to explain what had happened. I told her about Mrs. Gibbons's compromise, but I didn't mention Tad Gordon. She listened carefully before saying, "Honey, you don't have enough confidence in yourself, that's all. I'm sure that Christy would be happy to have your help. Good posters and stickers can make a big difference in a campaign like that. You'll just have to try not to be so shy. Take your portfolio, let her know you're serious about wanting to help, and everything will work out just fine. You'll see."

I sighed miserably. "I don't know, Mom," I said. "It's so hard for me to meet people. And, I'm afraid Christy will turn me down."

"You'll never know unless you try, honey," she said, starting toward the door.

After my mom had left, I looked in the mirror and studied my reflection. A mother's love was definitely blind. Sure, Christy and I both had long blond hair and blue eyes. We were probably about the same height, and our figures were more or less the same, too. But there were a million differences between Christy and me. Her smile had looked nice, though. I finally decided that maybe, just maybe, my mom was right. Christy probably would be happy to have some extra help with her campaign.

I saw Christy Monday morning in Senior Square, a special corner in the school court-yard. Since I was only a junior, I didn't normally hang out there, and I felt distinctly out of place. But I told myself that it didn't matter, and after working up all my courage, I walked over to Christy. I told her I was an advanced art student and that I would like to help with the artwork for her campaign. She looked at me, puzzled. "Do I know you?" she asked, a small frown creasing her forehead.

"Well, not really," I mumbled.

"Oh. I didn't think so. Well, listen, uh, Donna, it's really sweet of you to offer your help, but you know how you could help the most?" She turned on her dazzling cheer-leader smile. "Just vote for me on election day, and tell all your friends to vote for me, too. That would be a big help, and I'd really appreciate it."

"But what about your posters and stuff?" I asked.

"Hey, thanks so much for your offer, but my campaigns seem to work better when they're run by my good friends. It's sort of

14

like one big party that way." Christy flashed me a big phony smile. "You understand, right?" One of her cheerleader friends walked up to us then. "Oh, hi, Alice, this is, uh—" I could tell that she'd already forgotten my name.

"Donna. I was just leaving." They said nothing to stop me. I was so humiliated that I knew I wouldn't even be able to tell Sandy and Ellen what had happened. As it turned out, that didn't matter. They'd been having their own discussion of my problem.

Sandy slid into the seat next to mine at lunch. Every day she bought a chocolate shake and a chocolate doughnut, but somehow, she managed to stay thin. I always kidded her that her lunch fare was dull brown and visually uninteresting, but she always replied that she didn't care because it tasted great. That day, however, she wasn't talking about food, and neither was Ellen.

Ellen began. "Listen, Donna, we looked at this whole thing all wrong before. You should thank Mrs. Gibbons for giving you one of the rare opportunities of a lifetime. Why waste your time on Christy?"

"What are you talking about?" I asked. They must have been kidding.

"It's like this," Sandy explained. "We were

15

talking on the phone last night, and we suddenly realized that you have a perfect excuse to get to know Tad Gordon. I mean, how many junior girls would give just about anything to have a reason to work with a gorgeous senior boy almost every day?" She shook her head. "Honestly, you're so spaced out in that crazy art world of yours that you probably don't even know what he looks like. Well, wait till you see him."

My picture of Tad as the Roman god popped into my head, and I tried to keep my blush from heating up my face. Christy's rejection still stung, and I certainly didn't want to risk the same thing from Tad.

Sandy was still babbling on. "So, just walk right over to him at the end of lunch today and ask him. Just wait until he gets up from the table, and then sort of run into him by the door. He's right over there in the blue sweater—the third chair on the left." She turned to face me. "Oh, Donna, it will work out perfectly. I promise."

"Listen, you guys, I really appreciate all your help and everything, but I can't just march up to Tad and all his football friends and tell him he's got to let me do the art for his campaign."

"Well, then what *are* you going to do?" Sandy asked.

"I don't know." Almost to myself, I added, "If only I didn't have to talk to him face-to-face."

Sandy's eyes grew wide. "Donna, you don't have a crush on Tad, do you?"

"No," I answered a little too quickly. "Why on earth would you think that?"

Sandy shrugged and told me that no matter how I felt about Tad, I was crazy to let my whole art career be destroyed just because I was too scared to talk to him.

Sandy ended her lecture as the bell signaling the end of lunch period rang. I sighed, knowing that Sandy was right. I'd *have* to talk to Tad. I couldn't give up on the one thing I wanted most in the world, at least not without knowing that I'd given it my best shot. If only I weren't so shy! I knew that if I tried to talk to Tad, he'd think I was some kind of a tongue-tied idiot. On the other hand, if I didn't approach him soon, his campaign would be in full swing, and there'd be absolutely no point in saying anything at all.

Chapter Two

The afternoon passed uneventfully. After a dumb pop quiz in French and a lab assignment in science, the school day was finally over. I hadn't gotten a chance to talk to Tad once. After school, right when I was about to give up for the day, I did see him walking to his car. It even looked as though he were purposely walking slowly—as if he were expecting someone to come up to him. It was a perfect chance! Pushing my unwilling feet toward him, I prayed that he would at least consider using me to do the art for his campaign.

Fate seemed to be cooperating with me because, much to my delighted amazement, Tad look up just then and waved at me. At *me*! I started walking faster, and he kept looking in my direction. Soon, I was almost face-to-face with him. "Hi," I said in a squeaky voice.

"Well, hello." He smiled, but he looked a little confused. I was just about to mention my artwork when I realized that Tad was looking at me *and* at a girl who was standing behind me. Then the girl walked right past me.

"Tad," she said, "thanks for waiting for me. I had to talk to Mr. Cooper after class about my test. You're so sweet to give me a ride home," she added, linking her arm through his.

"Anytime. I'm everybody's dependable friend, right?" He grinned and the girl laughed. Meanwhile, I felt myself begin to turn bright red. The only thing I could do was leave as quickly as possible and hope I didn't die of embarrassment.

That night I called Sandy and told her all about it. "You know, now that I've thought it over, I'm sure that Tad never even looked at me at all. I think he must have been looking at the girl behind me the whole time. Sandy, he probably didn't even notice that I was there, and if he did, it was only to wonder who that nerdy girl was."

"I'm sure that's not true," Sandy assured

me. "You shouldn't have run off like that. He probably saw you and wondered why you left so quickly."

"But, Sandy," I argued, "that girl had her arm linked through his. Three *is* a crowd you know."

"And your art grade *does* depend on your getting up the nerve to talk to Tad, remember?"

"I don't want to talk about it anymore, OK?" I said. "It's just too depressing!" I flopped onto my bed and pulled a sketch pad from beneath it, quickly changing the subject. "So, what else is going on?"

"Well, in history today Mr. Anderson was telling us how America is the land of opportunity and all, and you know how he never stays on the subject. Well, pretty soon he was talking about how much opportunity there is to get involved in things here at Washington High and how important it is for as many students as possible to run for student-government positions. Then Allan Smythe—he's so gorgeous—raised his hand and said that it didn't make any difference who ran for office because the same kids always won anyway."

Sandy rambled on as usual, and as I listened, I started sketching a cartoon of Mr. Anderson. I over-accentuated his big, bushy eyebrows until they took up most of his forehead. When I was finished, I had to stifle a giggle. My drawing definitely looked like Mr. Anderson, but it certainly wasn't a portrait he would have been pleased to see. Briefly, I wondered what Mrs. Gibbons would think of my cartoon. If she saw it, maybe she would believe that my art *did* have life and humor. On the other hand, maybe she would send me to the dean for being disrespectful to a teacher.

Suddenly I realized that Sandy had stopped speaking and was waiting for me to say something. "Listen, Sandy, I'd better get going," I said, hoping she didn't think I was being too rude. "I mean, I'm just not very good company, and I don't want to put you in a bad mood, too."

"Don't be silly, Donna," Sandy replied. "What are friends for?" She paused before going on. "I know how you feel, though. Listen, I'll call you later, OK?"

"OK," I replied. After I put the receiver back in the phone cradle, I leaned back and stared up at the ceiling. *What have I gotten myself into?* I wondered. *And, how will I ever get out of this jam?* Knowing full well that there was only one way, I promised myself that I would talk to Tad in the morning, no matter what.

The next day I woke up hoping that something had magically changed during the night, but I knew nothing had. My life was still the same major mess, and there were only two possible solutions. Either I could corner Tad and beg him to let me do his artwork, or I could try to tell Mrs. Gibbons that I just couldn't do the project. Neither idea sounded very good. People like me did not hold regular conversations with people like Tad, and teachers like Mrs. Gibbons didn't give second chances very often. They probably never gave third chances at all.

I climbed out of bed and dressed for school as if I were getting ready to face a firing squad. All the way to school, I tried out imaginary conversations with Tad. "Hi, I know you don't know me, but my name is Donna Newbury, and I'm interested in doing the artwork for your campaign for student-body president." I shook my head. That sounded too negative—as though I was expecting to be turned down. I tried again. "Hi, today's your lucky day, Tad Gordon, because I'm volunteering to draw all your election posters."

Yuck. That sounded conceited and phony. I tried to think of something else, and before I knew it, I was at school. Practice time was over, too, because there in Senior Square was Tad Gordon.

Just do it, I told myself. *Just walk up to him and say something—anything!* Tad was talking to two or three guys, and I tried, but I just couldn't make myself approach a whole group of handsome senior boys. Instead, I waited in the background, hoping that maybe the other guys would eventually leave. When it seemed as though I had been waiting there forever, I looked at my watch; there were only two more minutes until the first bell rang. It was too late! Just when I was deciding that I was going to have to leave for class, I saw the other boys walk toward the main classroom building. Tad was now standing in Senior Square all by himself. Somehow, I'd gotten a second chance, and I wasn't going to blow it. I walked over to him quickly, before I could lose my nerve. All the things I had planned to say to him suddenly sounded ridiculous, and I couldn't think of anything that would make me appear witty and in control. In fact, Tad himself even seemed like a hazy blur as I stood in front of him. "Hi," I finally managed to squeak out. "I need to ask you a question."

It sounded dumb, I know, but at least I said something.

Tad looked at me quizzically. "OK, shoot," he said, shifting his books from one arm to the other. But as he did so, his expression became concerned. He looked down at his books and gasped, "Oh, no." Turning toward me, he apologized. "Look, I'm really sorry, but could we talk some other time? Brad Wilking just ran off with my bio book, and I'm dead if I show up in class without it." Not knowing what else to do, I nodded. "Oh, that's great. Hey, Brad!" he yelled, taking off after his friend. "Brad, wait up! I need my book."

That did it. I wasn't risking getting shot down again. Walking into art class later that morning, I plopped my books down on my desk and marched up to the front of the room. I hoped I could catch Mrs. Gibbons before class and tell her my problem. Unfortunately, Billy Adams beat me to her desk, carrying a large portfolio. It turned out that he needed to talk to her because he was having trouble getting the perspective right on a building in the painting he was working on. Mrs. Gibbons talked to him until the bell rang. Disappointed, I hurried to my seat. Now, I would have to get through another hour before I could talk to Mrs. Gibbons.

"Class," she called firmly, laying her glasses on her desk. "May I have your attention. Before we start on our batik projects, I'd like to show you some brochures I received yesterday from the Art Institute of America. Recently, I've learned more about this fine institution, and I'd like to share that knowledge with all of you today." Mrs. Gibbons looked directly at me and half smiled, but I looked away. Her smile would disappear when I told her I'd failed.

Mrs. Gibbons continued. "I like their philosophy so much that I plan to make a copy of it in calligraphy for our classroom. I want you all to listen." She opened the brochure and began reading: " 'The true artist lets nothing keep him from the canvas that must be completed. When his eye falters, his heart pushes him onward.' Who can explain that to me?"

Billy raised his hand. "It means that nothing can stop a true artist from completing a project he really cares about."

"That's exactly right." Mrs. Gibbons beamed. "And since this is an advanced art class, I want you all to keep that thought in mind before you come to me and tell me you're stuck on a project."

Oh, great! I thought. So much for expecting Mrs. Gibbons to understand. Either I talked Tad Gordon into using my talents or I would have to give up my chance to go to the finest art school in America and resign myself to being a nobody for the rest of my life.

Chapter Three

That night I lay in bed unable to sleep. It must have been about three in the morning when an idea suddenly hit me. It was absolutely perfect!

Sitting up, I turned on my nightstand light and pulled my sketch pad out from under the bed. Why hadn't I thought of it earlier? My pencil began racing across the paper as if it had a life of its own. After a few minutes of furious scribbling, I stopped to look at my work. Soon my bed was littered with crumpled balls of paper, and I still didn't have the clean lines I wanted. I began yet another sketch. This one was good, and I began to feel the same excitement that I always felt when a piece of artwork was going well. I held the pad away from me a bit to get a better look. It was finally just right. Wide-awake now, I got out of bed and began rummaging through my back pack. I pulled out two artist's pens, one bold red and the other bright blue, and carefully colored in my sketch to create a vivid, eye-catching poster. GORDON FOR A GREAT YEAR. The words stood out in bold graphics against the contemporary design behind them. It looked really professional. On a sheet of notebook paper I wrote, "Tad, my name is Donna Newbury. I'm a junior, and I'd really like to do the artwork for your student-body presidential campaign. Here is a sample of my work."

I put the note with the poster in a big manila envelope and wrote "Tad Gordon" on the outside. There was nothing more I could do until morning, but for the first time I began to think that this whole thing might work. After all, Tad didn't have to like me. He only had to like my work, and in my heart, I knew he would. I'd give him the poster, and if things went as planned, I wouldn't have to worry about talking to him.

The next morning I walked to school slowly. It was awkward carrying the large envelope, and two blocks from home, I wished I'd taken my artist's portfolio with the handle.

I got to school early and waited near Senior

Square, figuring that as soon as I saw Tad, I'd walk up to him, hand him the envelope, and run. Anxiously, I scanned the crowd of students, watching for each new arrival and wondering if I'd ever be as confident as those seniors. Somehow, I just couldn't see myself as anyone but shy, plain Donna Newbury.

The first bell rang, and I realized that I'd have to hurry to make it across campus before the tardy bell. *Darn!* I thought, lugging my backpack in one hand and the envelope in the other. Tad never showed up. Of course, I hadn't actually known if he hung out in Senior Square. I had just assumed he'd be there because Sandy said that was where you could find most of the popular seniors before school.

Hurrying to class, I wondered if Tad might be sick. That meant I'd have to haul the poster home and back again. Regretfully, I looked at my locker and wished I'd made the poster small enough to fit inside it. *Well, it's too late to worry about that now*, I thought, tearing toward class. Mr. Clausen, my first-period history teacher, got positively livid whenever students were late. I rounded the corner quickly and collided with a tall boy who was walking backward and calling to a friend. The impact almost knocked me off my feet.

"Hey, are you OK?"

It was none other than Tad Gordon. "Oh. I can't believe it's you," I said and then groaned inwardly. How could I have been so dumb? "Here." I thrust my envelope toward him before I could say anything else stupid and rushed off to class. By the time I sat down, I was starting to shake. Tad was even better looking in person than in my Roman god piece.

Instead of listening to Mr. Clausen's lecture, I thought about my unexpected encounter with Tad. It was a good thing I hadn't planned to say anything to him about working on his campaign. I'd already made a total fool of myself with the few words I did say. On the other hand, at least I had managed to get my artwork to him. That had been my goal, after all. He didn't have to like *me*. As long as Tad thought I was a good artist, everything would be fine.

At lunch I could hardly wait to see Sandy and Ellen. "Guess what, you guys?" I said as they joined me at the table I'd saved. I told them all about running into Tad. "Can you believe it? It's a good thing that poster didn't fit in my locker, or I'd never have had it with me."

Sandy's eyes grew serious. "Oh, that's not so surprising. I was reading your horoscope in last night's paper, and it said that good things were going to happen to Tauruses in the next day or two. Your horoscope is coming true, that's all."

"Gee, that's not bad," Ellen said. "What did mine say?"

"I don't know, I can't remember. I was concentrating on Donna's because she was so worried about her art project. *My* horoscope never says anything great. I guess Scorpios lead boring lives." Sandy frowned.

"Well, before my horoscope really comes true, Tad has to decide if he likes my poster and wants me to do his artwork," I reminded her.

"He will," replied Sandy confidently. "And when he does, you have to promise me that you'll introduce us to all his cute senior friends."

"Listen, Sandy," I began, exasperated, "don't get your hopes up, OK? Didn't you hear me say what a jerk I sounded like when I tried to talk to him? If he lets me do the art, I'm not going to say much of anything. I don't want to do a single thing that might make him want to fire me."

31

Sandy cocked one eye at me quizzically. "I hope you'll change your mind once you've worked with him for a while because I'm dying to go out with a cute senior guy!"

I laughed. Sandy was crazy sometimes, but she was also a terrific friend. "Maybe I could make a poster for you," I offered. "How about this: 'Wanted—one cute senior boy to date a desperate junior girl.'"

Sandy grinned. "If I thought it would work, I'd give it a try."

The next day I waited impatiently for Tad to let me know what he thought of my poster. I even made sure to hang out in places where he would be sure to find me—just outside Senior Square, in the front hallway of the school, even outside of his English classroom. But despite my best efforts, Tad never seemed to be where I was. By lunchtime I was so upset that I couldn't even eat. Nothing Sandy or Ellen could say made me feel even the least bit better. Then I spotted Tad across the cafeteria. I keep looking over at the table where he was sitting with his friends, and the more I watched him, the angrier I got. How dare he mess up everything for me and then sit over there laughing as if it didn't matter at all? The least he could have done was say that it

32

was nice of me to draw the poster, but no thanks. I'd spent almost two hours on it, slaving away in the middle of the night while he had probably been sound asleep. And the poster was good, or I thought it was anyway.

I watched Tad get up to return his lunch tray. I honestly don't know how I got there, but all of a sudden, I was standing right next to him. A voice was coming out of my mouth saying angrily, "Even if you didn't like the poster I made for you, you could have at least returned it."

Tad looked confused. "What are you talking about? Have we met?"

Then I realized where I was and who I was speaking to. "No, uh, no, I don't think we have. I'm Donna Newbury."

"Oh," said Tad slowly. I could feel his eyes looking me over. "I'm Tad Gordon."

"I know that," I said, feeling stupider than ever. "I, um, gave you that big envelope in the hall yesterday."

"Envelope? What envelope?"

My anger flashed again. "You mean you don't even remember me? You practically ran me down yesterday, and I gave you a big art folder. Don't you remember?"

"Oh, that. Geez, I completely forgot. Oh, I'm really sorry. You know, I was late for Spanish, and I tore in just as Senor Erlhy was telling everyone to clear their desks for a test. By the time I'd finished the test, I was going to be late for my next class, too. I just grabbed my books and took off. I, uh, guess the folder must still be in the Spanish room. I never even opened it. Why'd you give it to me, anyway?"

All of a sudden I noticed that Tad Gordon's eyes were an even deeper shade of blue than I'd thought they were. I took a deep breath and prayed that I wasn't going to start blushing. The worst part about being so fair was that when I blushed, everyone could see the red, even in the part in my hair. "Well, uh, I wanted to work on the posters for your campaign. You know, coordinate the art and stuff. I figured you didn't know who I was, so I thought I'd show you a sample of what I could do. That's what was in the folder."

Tad's dark eyebrows arched questioningly. "And why would you want to do the art for my campaign?"

I wished more than anything in the world that I could come up with one of those clever responses that the heroines in books always seemed to have ready. Instead, I just said, "Because I like to draw, and I think it would be fun."

"I was hoping it was because you think I'm a terrific candidate," he said very seriously. But I could see the laughter in his eyes. "Or because you think that I'm so incredibly handsome that you just couldn't stay away."

I felt a dreaded blush spreading across my face. Tad noticed and grinned. "I'll tell you what, Donna. We've still got five minutes of lunch hour left, so let's go by the Spanish room and see what kind of an artist you really are."

"Oh, I don't have to come," I said quickly. "I mean, you can just look when you . . ." I felt a strong hand on my arm as Tad headed us in the direction of the door.

"Doesn't every artist attend the opening of her own show?" he said.

The cafeteria spun in a haze as we pushed our way through the crowd and into the hall. I thought for a minute that I saw Sandy still sitting at our table, openmouthed, but everything was so blurry that I couldn't be sure.

I didn't even try to make small talk as we walked to the Spanish room. Instead, I worried that my poster might not be there, and then I worried that it would. Maybe he'd see the poster and not like it at all. On top of everything else, I was so nervous about walking with such a cute guy that I was afraid I might trip over my own feet and fall flat on my face or something.

The door squeaked as we walked into the empty room. Tad went immediately to a desk by the window. "It's still here," he called, reaching down for something. "Right where I left it. Well, Donna, are you ready for the official unveiling of your creation?"

My feet were frozen to the ground, and I couldn't look at him as he carefully pulled the poster from the envelope. The silence in the room seemed to go on forever. Finally Tad spoke. "Hey, this is really good. How come I never heard anything about you before?" I shrugged, embarrassed, but Tad didn't seem to notice. "Usually, I'm pretty much of an expert on good-looking girls—especially ones who blush easily."

Mercifully, the bell rang, saving me from having to come up with some kind of response. My face was probably deep purple by then. "Geez," Tad said in surprise. "I'd better get moving. If I'm late for PE, old Smith will make me do fifty push-ups." Heading quickly toward the door, he called over his shoulder, "Hey, Donna, you've got yourself a job as my campaign art coordinator. I'll call you tonight, OK? Are you in the phone book?"

Totally stunned by how things had turned

out, I managed only a half whisper. "Yeah, my dad's first name is George."

"OK." With a grin, Tad turned and started weaving rapidly through the students in the crowded hallway.

I stood there wondering whether I'd ever be able to move from the room. I could just see Senor Erlhy coming in to start class and finding me rooted to that exact spot. I laughed out loud in relief. *This has got to be one of the very best days of my entire life*, I thought. I finally got going and made it to my next class just in time.

I could hardly wait until after school to tell Sandy and Ellen what had happened. I hoped I'd be able to catch them before they started home, but I needn't have worried. They were both hovering over my locker waiting for me to tell them everything.

"You are absolutely amazing," Ellen said. "One minute you're sitting in the cafeteria complaining that your whole art career is down the tubes, and the next minute you're disappearing from the cafeteria with everyone's dream guy."

"Tell us every little detail," Sandy ordered. "Don't you dare leave out one single thing. No, wait. Don't start yet. An event this monumental deserves our full attention. What do you say we go to Swensen's for milk shakes?"

Soon, we were seated at the ice-cream and hamburger shop down the block from school. As soon as the waitress had set three tall chocolate milk shakes before us, Sandy insisted, "Now tell us *all* about it."

Stirring the straw around my creamy shake, I tried to find the best way to tell them about Tad. "Honest, you guys, I don't really know how I had the guts to go talk to him. I think I got mad because my whole life was getting ruined, and he didn't even have the courtesy to say yes or no to my poster proposal. For a minute I forgot who he was, or else I just didn't care. I wanted to let him know that I thought he was a jerk, you know what I mean?" I stopped a minute and took a big sip of my milk shake. "None of this is making much sense, is it? Everything happened so fast, and I was so surprised at what I'd done, that I can't remember a lot of the details. I guess I was in shock."

"Then just tell us what he said," Sandy urged impatiently, her green eyes gleaming in anticipation. "How did things end up?"

My heart practically sang the answer. "I get to work on Tad's campaign! He said I could be his art director."

Both Ellen and Sandy were really happy for me, but their mouths dropped open when I added, "He's going to call me tonight, too."

"I can't believe it," Sandy squealed. "My friend who's so shy she can't even talk to the pizza delivery boy has managed to get the most popular guy at Washington High interested in her in just a few minutes! Where do we sign up for lessons?"

"Oh, come on, you guys," I protested, laughing. "He doesn't care about me at all. And that's OK—at least he thinks I'm a good artist. That's what really counts."

Sandy stared at me so intently that I had to look away. "Donna," she said softly, "even the most famous artists in the world have something in their lives besides their work."

Chapter Four

Although I'd shrugged off Sandy's comment, her words lingered in my mind as I walked home. Since I'd moved to Tucson, I hadn't had a boyfriend. In fact, I'd never really had a boyfriend at all. There had been fewer than two hundred kids in our entire high school back in Yankton, and we'd known one another all our lives. There wasn't much romance at the school dances, but then there wasn't much social pressure, either. Everybody knew everybody else too well.

When I got home, I grabbed a snack and sat down at the kitchen table to try to come up with some clever poster ideas. It wasn't going to be easy, working so closely with Tad Gordon. My dad always told me that I shouldn't be so shy about talking to boys. "They're just as nervous as you are," he had said again and again. Then he'd wink at my mom. "I ought to know. Once upon a time, I was a jittery kid, too." My parents seemed to find that hilariously funny, and it frequently started them reminiscing about how they'd met or about their first date. I never really listened to the whole story since I'd learned it by heart long before. Besides, even though I knew my dad loved me and believed what he was saying, his advice was no good. I had this theory about parents, which Sandy and Ellen agreed with entirely. After parents had children of their own, they didn't remember much about being a kid. That was why my dad wouldn't understand that guys like Tad Gordon weren't shy at all, especially with shy, average girls like me.

I looked down at my blank sketch pad. I hadn't drawn a single thing. "Tad Gordon." I tried the letters in calligraphy, but that didn't suit him at all. There was nothing frilly about Tad. I scratched out the lettering and stared at the page once again. I had hoped to have five or six different ideas by the time he called. So far, the bold, bright block lettering that I'd done for the sample poster still seemed the best.

The phone rang. My stomach turned upside down, and my mouth felt like cotton. "If that's for me," I called to my mom, "say I haven't gotten home yet." I wasn't sure if she'd heard me. I waited a few minutes, just to be safe, and then rushed downstairs and into the kitchen.

"Who was on the phone?" My voice came out in a squeak.

"Donna, are you OK, honey? You look a little pale."

"I'm fine, Mom," I replied, forcing a smile. "Was, uh, that for me?"

"No, it was a solicitation to buy a solar water heater. Why? Are you expecting some special call?"

I considered explaining the whole thing to her, and then I thought of how I might have to hear another of my dad's pep talks. I knew I couldn't handle that right then, so I just shrugged. "No, not really. I may be doing some work on an election campaign at school, and someone is supposed to call me about it."

That seemed to satisfy my mother, who appeared to have forgotten our conversation about Christy. Before she could ask me any more questions, I said that I really had a lot of homework and that I'd better go back to my room and get started. I was almost out the door when she called to me. I turned around, not sure what to expect. "I'm glad you're getting involved in your new school," she said. "You have a lot to offer, honey."

"Thanks, Mom," I said. "I'm trying." I knew my parents still felt bad about taking me away from all my friends in South Dakota. On the way to my room, I thought about how lucky I was that I got along so well with my mom and dad. Some kids always fought with their parents about everything. I was glad that even though I didn't always agree with mine, I never doubted for a moment how much they loved me.

By eight o'clock that night, Sandy and Ellen had both called twice. My heart banged in my chest each time the phone rang, and my throat had practically closed off whenever my mom or dad had yelled that it was for me.

"Maybe he's busy or something and can't get to a phone," Sandy suggested when she called for about the millionth time. "He'll probably try you tomorrow, so don't be so nervous."

But as hard as I tried, I just couldn't take Sandy's advice and calm down. My stomach stayed full of butterflies as I nervously paced around the room.

Noticing my algebra book, which was still lying untouched on my bed, I reluctantly picked it up. I wished that my assignment could somehow get done by itself. But, it couldn't. Picking up a pencil, I began to work, but I couldn't remember how to set up the equation for the first story problem. Fortunately, math was so confusing that I had to concentrate completely to get it straight. All my thoughts about Tad and art were momentarily replaced by x's and y's.

At nine o'clock the phone rang once again. Glancing at my watch, I grinned. Sandy was right on cue, and I was more than ready for a break from algebra. I picked up the phone next to my bed. "No, I haven't heard anything yet, and your call is thirty-two seconds late!"

"Uh, is this Donna Newbury's house?" A deep male voice came from the other end of the phone.

I would have gladly let the floor swallow me up right there on the spot. Nothing happened, though, and the voice on the other end of the phone had to be answered. I said the first thing that came to mind. "Oh, yes, this is her cousin. I'll get her."

I put the phone down quickly. "Donna," I called, "It's for you!" Crossing my fingers that my parents wouldn't walk in and ask why I was shouting to myself, I waited a few seconds and picked up the receiver. Only I could mess up a phone call before it had even begun.

"Hello," I said, trying to make my voice sound a little different than it had before.

"Hi, Donna, this is Tad." He seemed friendly enough, but I wasn't going to take any more chances on sounding like an idiot.

Skip the small talk, I told myself. *You were never much good at it anyway.* "Oh, hi, Tad. Let me get a pen and some paper so I can take notes on what kinds of posters and buttons you want, OK?"

"Wow, Miss Efficiency!" There was a teasing tone in Tad's voice, and I couldn't tell if he was making fun of me or just kidding around.

The best thing to do, I decided, was to simply ignore the comment. "All right, I'm ready," I said. I forced myself to forget that this was Tad Gordon, Washington High superhunk. Instead, I made myself imagine that I was talking to old Mr. Allenson, the head of the local retired veterans group back in Yankton. "Now," I continued briskly, "if you'll give me some ideas for what you want and when you want it, I'll be able to plan a schedule for us. Oh, and do you want to approve everything yourself as I sketch it, or should I just give you the finished pieces?"

There was silence on the other end of the phone. "Uh, Donna, you haven't worked on many student campaigns around here, have you?"

I began to twirl my hair nervously. "No, actually this is my first one," I said. Then I realized that I probably shouldn't have admitted how inexperienced I was. Tad probably didn't want some person who'd never worked on a campaign before. Clearing my throat, I added, "Of course, I worked on lots of them back in South Dakota." He didn't have to know that my school was tiny and that the elections were nothing compared to the ones at Washington. "I know how important posters and buttons are in getting votes."

Tad laughed, but it didn't sound as if he were making fun of me. "Hey, Donna, this is just for student-body president, not president of the country. I'll tell you what, Miss Efficiency. We're going to have a campaign meeting at my house tomorrow night. Why don't you come over about eight, and together we should all be able to answer your questions then. Oh, and you can bring some tapes along if you want. We think best with good music and lots of junk food."

I panicked. No way was I ready to get together with the most popular crowd in the

46

school. I'd never fit in with all those kids. "Oh, uh, thanks," I said, trying to sound enthusiastic, "but I've already got plans for tomorrow night." It was a lie, but I couldn't let Tad know I was too nervous to go to his house.

"Friday night date, huh? I might have guessed. Well, bring the guy along. Our parties are usually pretty good, not too wild or anything."

I took a deep breath. What had I gotten myself into now? I couldn't bring a date to Tad's party since I'd made the whole thing up. I didn't even have a possible prospect for a date. "You know," I said quickly, "I'm sure your party will be great, but I just can't make it this time."

"Too bad," he replied, and I could have sworn that there was really a note of regret in his voice. "Well, we'll try to get a few things decided tomorrow night. I'll give you a call and let you know about it, OK? Talk to you later."

The phone went dead. Right away I walked over to the mirror on my dresser to make sure that I hadn't undergone some sort of transformation. No, I was still the same plain Donna Newbury. I went back to the bed to start tackling my homework problems again, but it was impossible to concentrate. Tossing the algebra aside, I decided to call Sandy. "You'll never believe what just happened to me!" I said as soon as she answered.

"Tad called," she guessed. "See, I told you—"

"Yes," I cut in excitedly, "but that's not all. He actually asked me to come to a party at his house tomorrow night. Can you believe that?"

"Oh, wow!" Sandy gasped in amazement. "You've got to keep track of every detail of the whole evening, and you have to call me by ten o'clock Saturday morning. Maybe you'll even meet some of Tad's friends, and you can fix Ellen and me up with them. Then, we can all go to the next party! Wouldn't that be something?"

"Sandy, I'm not going to the party."

It wasn't usually easy to shut Sandy up, but that did it. In fact, it was so quiet on the other end of the phone that I wasn't sure Sandy was still there. "Sandy?"

"Oh, Donna, I don't believe it," she groaned. "Why didn't you say yes?"

"I don't know," I answered miserably. "I was too chicken, I guess. It doesn't matter, anyway. I couldn't possibly have a good time with all those popular kids."

Sandy groaned and then she hung up on me.

As I sat at home on Friday night watching reruns on television, I began to wish I had gone to Tad's. I played a dumb little game with myself, checking the clock every twenty minutes or so and trying to figure out what was going on at the party. "It's just as well I didn't go," I told myself. "I wouldn't have fit in anyway." But, sitting around feeling sorry for myself wasn't going to help. "Miami Vice" came on and I decided to draw Don Johnson during the show. I pulled out a small sketch pad, and soon I was absorbed in watching the actor's movements. It was hard, trying to capture all the action in a still sketch, but I was pleased with my efforts.

See, I told myself. *This is much more interesting than trying to have fun with a bunch of kids I've never met.* I knew none of my friends would agree with that statement, and somehow, I wasn't quite sure I believed it myself.

Chapter Five

I had gone to bed late on Friday night, so as soon as I heard my alarm ring the next morning, I groaned and reached over to turn it off. On the one day I could sleep late, I wasn't going to get out of bed early. Opening one eye, I saw that my clock read eleven-thirty. Why had I set the alarm at all? Yawning, I buried my head in my pillow and went back to sleep. The next thing I knew, there was a knock at my door. "Donna," my mother called. She was standing in the doorway. "Are you awake?"

"I guess I am now," I replied groggily.

"Well, good!" My mom was smiling. "There's a young man named Tad Gordon waiting to see you in the family room. He looks like a very nice boy, Donna."

I sat up quickly. "Tad Gordon is here? In *our* family room?" I asked aghast.

"Yes, dear, that's what I said. Shall I tell him you'll be down in a few minutes? It's after noon."

"In our family room," I repeated.

"Donna," my mom said firmly, "I really think you should get dressed. After all, it would be rude to make Tad wait too long."

"But what am I going to say to him?" I asked, panicked.

"Now, Donna, your father always says—"

"Right, Mom, I know." I couldn't stand the thought of hearing that whole thing again right now. My stomach was doing nervous flip-flops, and I had to figure out something to wear. "I'll be down soon, OK?"

I glanced longingly at the phone. Maybe I could call Sandy and see if she had some ideas on what Tad and I might talk about. I got as far as picking up the receiver, but then I reconsidered and put it down again. Unless I could bring the phone with me into the family room and check with her after every comment, there was no point in calling. Besides, I had no idea what I was going to wear.

I dove into my closet and started pulling out practically every piece of clothing I owned.

The green turtleneck I'd gotten for my birthday made me look sallow, and I noticed that my favorite red shirt had a spot in the front. Finally I settled on a long, ribbed royal-blue sweater, which I figured would look casual enough for a Saturday afternoon. I looked all over the room for my new jeans, but they were no where to be found. Unfortunately, I didn't have time to look for them, so I settled on another pair of jeans. Hurriedly I pulled a brush through my hair. I'd worn it parted on the side and straight ever since I was a little girl. Lately I'd been thinking about cutting it short, so I'd look more sophisticated, and now I wished I'd kept that appointment with Ellen's hairdresser. I'd canceled it at the last minute, after deciding that it would take years to grow my hair long again if I didn't like it short.

"Just another example of what a chicken you are," I told myself, frowning into the mirror. At least my face wasn't broken out. I grabbed an eye shadow that picked up the color of the blue sweater and lined my eyes expertly. I'd always loved playing with makeup. Painting a face was another form of art, as far as I was concerned. I lined my lips carefully with pink rose and filled them in. After adding a touch of matching blush to my cheeks, I stood back to survey my reflection. Briefly I thought about putting on pearls with my sweater, but I decided that the look would be all wrong. Nobody wore pearls on a Saturday afternoon but the sweater still needed something. Frantically I scanned my closet once again until I noticed my wide red belt. I slipped it on and let it slide low over one hip. Perfect.

I checked myself in the mirror one last time. *That's it,* I thought. *I've got to go downstairs and face Tad.* I'd certainly never be Christy Jenkins, but I looked about as good as I could, for me. I glanced at the clock on my nightstand. My mom had come in almost fifteen minutes before, and who knew how many questions my dad had already asked Tad. My dad was such a tease, and we hadn't had enough boys around our house to have had the chance to work out what was and wasn't OK for him to say. Sighing deeply, I pushed myself toward the door. Sooner or later I'd have to see my dad and Tad, and the longer I left them alone together, the worse things might get.

Fortunately, when I walked into the family room, they weren't talking at all. There was some basketball game on the TV, and they didn't even notice my entrance. "Will you look at that!" my father suddenly yelled. "That's the third free throw he's missed! What's the matter with him?"

"I don't know," said Tad in a disgusted tone. "I do know the Arizona State coaches think he's really hot, especially when you consider that he's only a sophomore. But he sure looks terrible today."

"Uh, hi," I said. Tad certainly looked terrific. He was dressed casually in jeans and a tan sweater. He looked like one of the male models in *Seventeen*.

"Shh," my dad said. "Donna, don't interrupt. There are only three minutes left, and this thing keeps seesawing back and—Oh, no! Did you see that shot? What a risk! He must have made that thing from midcourt!"

Tad looked away from the TV for maybe ten seconds. "Hi," he said and then he turned right back to the tube.

Great, I thought to myself. *What a terrific start. Well, it serves me right for getting off the track on this art project. Tad Gordon means nothing to me, so I don't care that he's more interested in watching basketball with my father than he is in talking to me.* I reconsidered. *OK, so maybe I am a tiny bit upset. But it's only because I rushed so much to get ready. They could at least have let me know they were going to be so totally ab-sorbed in this stupid basketball game.*

I stood in the back of the room and waited until the end of the regulation game and then through two overtimes. After that I listened to them discuss what they'd just seen. Finally I thought about leaving to go shopping or something. They probably wouldn't even have noticed.

At last it seemed to dawn on them that I was in the room. "Wasn't that an exciting game, honey?" my dad said.

"Sorry if we got carried away," Tad apologized, "but that had to be the best game Arizona State has played all season." I had a feeling he was about to launch into another discussion of why with my dad, but strangely enough, neither my dad or Tad said anything further. Both of them looked at me, and all of a sudden I wished that they were still talking about basketball.

My dad awkwardly cleared his throat, as if he realized for the first time that a boy had come to see his daughter. "Well, I've got some things to do," he said. "Nice meeting you, Tad." With that, he left the room.

Tad turned a ten-megawatt smile on me. "Hey, you look great today! You know your dad's a real nice guy. That was some game."

He leaned back on the sofa as if he felt perfectly at home there, and my heart began to pound. I knew I should sit down, too, but I felt a little weak at the thought of being that close to Tad.

Perching on the edge of the sofa, I searched for something to say. "I'm—uh—sorry that I couldn't come to your party last night."

"No problem," Tad replied. "There'll be lots more before this election is over. To tell you the truth, it isn't going to be easy to beat Christy." For the first time since I'd met him, I saw a worried frown cross his face. "I mean, I'm not expecting this to be a shoo-in election or anything." I was just about to say that I was sure he'd win, but he looked over at me and grinned. "Then again, we've got *you* on our side."

Blushing, I tried to get the conversation moving toward art. At least I'd be on safer ground there. "So, did anybody get a chance to look at the poster I made for you?"

"Yeah," Tad said. "As a matter of fact, lots of the kids saw it. Everyone thinks you are a dynamite artist."

"Really?" I asked, fishing a little.

"Really!" He laughed and then became serious. "But, Donna, everyone had the same feeling I did. The poster is great, but it just isn't me."

"Oh." I tried not to feel let down. I'd thought the strong, bold lines fit him perfectly.

Tad stretched his long arms out across the back of the sofa, and his hand grazed my shoulder. It sent chills up and down my back. The gesture was probably an accident, though, because the next minute Tad was on his feet, pacing back and forth.

"Let me give you a little background on this whole situation," he began. "Then maybe you'll understand everything better. I guess you could say that, basically, the same few of us have been involved in student government at Washington High since about ninth grade. Christy and I have gone head to head more than once, and the results have been pretty much even. I guess I'd always hoped to finish my senior year as student-body president, especially after Christy had said she didn't plan to run." Tad shrugged his broad shoulders and attempted a half grin. "Obviously she changed her mind. Anyway, most of the kids at school don't really care which one of us wins. So, how will they decide who to vote for? Maybe they'll have a friend whose friend is a friend of ours, but mostly they're going to judge by whose campaign is the funniest or the most unique. We need something to grab their attention. And that's where you come in." Tad stopped pacing and let his eyes travel from my feet to the top of my head.

"What do you mean?" I asked nervously, unable to meet his gaze.

"Well, in the past we've focused on doing skits, giving out cookies or pieces of candy, writing speeches to songs and songs to speeches. But posters—no one's ever done much with them. Oh, sure, you have to have something, slap up a bunch of signs with your name on them. That's the way we've always treated posters." Tad's voice grew excited. "But then a terrific artist like you comes along, and we have a different ball game. You're the key to making this year's campaign different—slick, professional artwork that really makes everyone sit up and take notice!" He winked as if we were co-conspirators.

I didn't even realize that Tad had brought my poster back to me. He must have put it beside the sofa when he'd come in. "Look," he said, pointing at the poster, "and tell me what you see."

"Oh, come on Tad." I squirmed uncomfortably. "I drew it, remember?"

"OK, OK. Maybe that's not a fair request. Let me get right to my idea. Donna, can you draw cartoons?"

I thought of my most recent one, the caricature of Mr. Anderson, bushy eyebrows and all. No one knew about my cartoons. I'd never considered them appropriate for someone who wanted to be serious about art. They'd just been fun to draw. "Well," I said, stalling while I thought, "I suppose I could try one."

"Great! I knew you'd be able to. Donna, don't you see? Your cartoons will be the focus of my whole campaign. We could have a continuing comic strip on the big wall outside the library. Who doesn't like to read the comics?" Tad's eyes were sparkling. "I got so keyed up thinking about this, I could hardly wait to get over here and talk to you this morning. Think you could try a sample one?"

My eyes grew wide. "Now? You want me to draw a cartoon now?" All I could think of was how nervous I'd be trying to draw with Tad looking over my shoulder.

He drew in a sharp breath. "Hey, I'm sorry, Donna. I guess I was really out of line." He bit his lip and his face clouded uneasily. "I've been a real jerk, just barging in here and expecting your time. I'll tell you what. Whenever you think you could get one done, let me know. I'll give you my phone number. You don't have to color them in or anything. Some of the rest of us will do that. But do you, uh, have any idea when you might be able to start on the first one?"

A smile pulled at the corners of my mouth. He looked so sweet and somehow vulnerable in spite of all that rugged handsomeness. "How about right now?" I heard myself say.

Tad's face split into a wide grin. "You mean it?"

"Sure. Wait here while I go get my pencils and some paper, OK?"

There was an excited gleam in Tad's eyes. "Hey, Donna," he said, his voice low and rich, "you're really one terrific girl."

Feeling flustered, but happier than I could ever remember being, I headed for my room to get my art supplies. As I caught my reflection in the mirror on the way out the door, I saw a glow in my cheeks that the best blusher in the world couldn't have put there. I smiled at my image and wished that the day would never end.

Chapter Six

When I first spread out my art materials on the kitchen table, my fingers felt a little stiff. I wasn't sure I'd be able to draw with Tad standing behind me and looking right over my shoulder. But after the first few minutes, we really started discussing the cartoon panels, and my shyness gave way to total absorption in the figures I was drawing.

"I think I still look too normal in that one," Tad said. "Can you exaggerate my features more? I want kids to look at these posters and laugh."

"OK," I said tentatively. I couldn't imagine having enough confidence in myself to invite people to laugh at me. "What do you think I should exaggerate?"

"Oh, I don't know. I've got a pretty square jaw. Why don't you make it even wider?"

I allowed myself the luxury of carefully examining his handsome face. His jaw looked perfect to me, but I tried to do as he had suggested. He bent over me, and I was very aware of how close he was. *He's only here to have you draw posters,* I reminded my singing heart.

I sketched and resketched until we finally had a silly caricature that was clearly recognizable as Tad. "Perfect," he pronounced, holding up the last one I had drawn. "Meet Tad the Terrific." He put the sketch next to his face. "Looks just like me, don't you think?"

"Oh, no, you're much better looking." My hand flew to my mouth. I hadn't meant to say that out loud. A brilliant blush rapidly covered my face.

I couldn't bring myself to look at Tad, but it was clear from the tone in his voice that he was amused. "Thanks for the compliment," he said. "You look pretty nice yourself. I like that blue sweater."

"Uh, who do you think we should have as the other characters in the cartoon?" I asked, fighting another creeping blush.

Tad looked at me and smiled. "How about a girl with long blond hair who turns red easily?"

His words only made me blush more furiously. At that moment my mother walked into the kitchen. "Hey, you two, I think you both missed lunch long ago," she said. "I've got some salami for sandwiches if you'd like."

Tad said he thought that sounded great. I made the sandwiches quickly, and we sat eating without saying much. Then Tad casually said, "This was terrific. Next time we'll go out."

I let my mind drift for a minute, imagining Tad and me sitting in the pizza place by school. His arm was wrapped securely around my shoulder, and he was telling people how we'd first met months before when I'd volunteered to work on his campaign. The other popular kids at our booth were telling us that we made a perfect couple. . . .

"Hey, did you hear a word I just said?" I looked up, startled, and Tad grinned. "I guess that answers my question." He shrugged his powerful shoulders nonchalantly. "Maybe we need a break. Why don't you come over to my house for a meeting tomorrow? We could work out the rest of the characters for the comic strip then."

"Oh, that's OK," I said a shade too quickly. Trying to cover myself I added, "We have a lot to do and not that much time, so I think we should get at least one other character done today."

63

Tad laughed a deep, throaty chuckle and placed a firm hand on my shoulder. "That's my girl!"

Those words sounded wonderful, and I wished they were really true. I couldn't say that, of course, so I turned all-business again and reviewed our plan. "OK, so we've got you as the superhero, and we've decided you should have a sidekick."

"Right. Any ideas?" Tad looked at me almost pleadingly. "I'm stuck on this one."

A picture suddenly began to form in my mind, and I grabbed a green pen and started to draw. Tad tried to watch over my shoulder, and once again, having him so close made my nerves tingle. I made him promise he wouldn't look until I was done. I tried to draw quickly and made one mistake after another. Finally I sent Tad to the family room so I could concentrate. I could hear that my dad had turned on another TV sports program. I kept drawing figures until one looked good to me. I held up my finished picture of Tad the Terrific with a funny version of our school mascot, the Washington Warrior, running after him. "There," I told myself, "is the perfect sidekick for our school's superhero."

I was so excited that I hurried toward the family room to show my drawing to Tad. As I rounded the corner, I stopped in the doorway to observe his profile without being seen. A lock of wavy dark hair had fallen onto his forehead, and his strong hands were resting firmly on his knees. Neither he nor my dad spoke, and I thought that I might just stand there for a while, admiring Tad without having to make conversation. But afraid that he'd turn and catch me staring at him like some little kid with a crush, I walked into the room and announced that I was done.

Tad and my father looked up from the TV screen as I revealed my sketch with a flourish. *"Ta-da!"*

"Hey," said my dad in surprise, "that's very clever, Donna. I don't think I've ever seen you draw anything like that before."

"Well," I began, looking at the piece more critically, "maybe it's a little too corny."

"Are you kidding?" Tad cut in, jumping up from the sofa. "I love it! It's going to win me the election!"

Tad suggested we go into the kitchen again so we wouldn't disturb my dad and the game. I could tell that his mind was racing.

We'd no sooner walked through the swinging doors of the kitchen than Tad began. "You're brilliant! I don't know why I didn't think of making the school mascot my side-kick. It's all going to work perfectly! Of course, we'll have to think up some silly story lines to go with the characters, but that shouldn't be hard. Each day, just like the soaps everyone loves to watch on TV, we'll have another installment of our comic strip. Can't you see it?" Tad stood and brushed his hand through the air. "Tad the Terrific and the Washington Warrior battle the Homework Menace, the Teacher Toughs, and the Student Blahs. Will school spirit return? Will students have a chance to abolish homework? Tune in tomorrow for the next installment of 'Tad the Terrific.' "

Tad, looking a bit embarrassed, took the sketch from my hands. "Yeah, it's corny, but it's OK. It's fun, and I've really got a feeling that it's going to be the talk of Washington High. And it's all thanks to you."

He reached over, and I was almost sure he was going to hug me, when he happened to look at the kitchen clock.

"Four-thirty! Wow! What happened to Saturday? Boy, I hope I can find a florist to work on short notice, or I'm dead!" A frown creased his face. "What would *you* do if your date showed up for the dance at school tonight without a corsage?" He immediately held up his hand in protest. "No, on second thought, don't answer that. I don't want to know."

He needn't have worried. I certainly wasn't

66

going to tell someone as popular as Tad that I didn't have to worry about getting a corsage because I hadn't even been asked to the winter formal. Until Tad mentioned the dance, I had almost been able to forget about it.

Tad started to pick up the sketches I had done, but then he put them back down on the table again. "Why don't you hang on to these until tomorrow? After all, they're your creations. You ought to have the honor of presenting them."

"Tomorrow?" I was unable to keep up with his rapidly changing thoughts.

An infectious grin spread once again across Tad's lips. "Oh, yeah, I forgot you weren't there last night. We're having another campaign meeting at my house tomorrow night at seven. If you need a ride, I'll come get you. I'd really like you to be there."

"You would?" I inhaled sharply.

"Absolutely," he assured me. "Your art is going to be the cornerstone of my campaign, right? Who could better explain it than you?"

I managed a weak smile and avoided Tad's eyes. This was exactly everything I'd wanted, I told myself, but there was some small part of me that hoped he wanted me to come to his house because he liked to be with me. "Well, I'm not sure how long I can stay," I replied, hedging. "But I'll be there at seven."

"Great!" Tad turned and headed for the door. As I let him out, he added casually, "See you tonight. Tell your date that I'm planning to steal you for a slow dance—if it's OK with you, I mean." Without waiting for an answer, he started briskly down the walk. When he got to the sidewalk's edge, he gave me a thumbs-up sign and climbed into his dark-blue car.

The car sped off as I shut the door. Practically floating up to my room, I envisioned Tad asking me to dance. I could almost feel myself in his arms, his fingers running gently through my hair as I rested my head on his shoulder.

The phone rang, bursting the bubble of my beautiful daydream. I frowned and picked up the receiver. "Donna? Is Tad still there? If so, I'll call back later."

"He just left, Sandy. How did you even know he was here?"

Giggling, she replied, "Oh, I called your house this morning to see if you wanted to go to the mall or something today, and your mom happened to mention it. I told her not to interrupt you. I've been thinking about you all day long. So—I'm listening. Let's hear everything."

Although I couldn't see Sandy, I'd have been willing to bet that she was lying on the floor with her feet up on her bed. That was her favorite position for long phone conversations.

I began to tell her about Tad's unexpected visit, trying to keep all traces of the excitement I'd felt out of my voice. There was no point in letting myself or Sandy think that I really had a chance with a boy like Tad. But in spite of my careful narration, Sandy was excited enough for both of us. She interrupted me about every third word. "Geez, he's really nice. He's not stuck-up or anything at all. I think maybe he likes you. If you'd given Harold Waltzan even a tiny bit of encouragement, he'd have asked you to the dance tonight, and then you'd get to see Tad. You're always so darn shy. How about if I fixed you up with my cousin Herman? That way you could go to the dance, and Tad could cut in."

"Sandy!" I exclaimed.

"OK," she said quickly. "So maybe it's not such a good idea. Herman's kind of a geek, and besides, the dance is formal. What would you wear? But at least I'm trying to figure out something. Even if you're not at the dance tonight, Tad assumed you were going, and that means he thinks you're popular! I just *know* he must like you. Why else would he have given up his whole Saturday to be with you?"

"Sandy," I interrupted, "hold on a minute." I couldn't let her go on that way. I didn't want to have my hopes built up for nothing. It would only leave me open for a bad heartache. "Tad probably thinks everyone is going to the dance," I said. "And he spent his whole Saturday with me because he thinks my drawings can help him get elected student-body president. I'm really happy that he thinks I can do the job, and I'm glad that he's nice. I'd hate to have to work on some conceited jerk's campaign, just so I could improve my grade in Mrs. Gibbons's class." Hoping to change the subject, I added, "Hey, what did you get at the mall today?"

Sandy began to tell me in great detail about trying to decide between a pair of black cords and red stirrup pants. "I wish you'd been there to give me advice," she said.

We talked for almost an hour before my mom came in and said that the phone would soon be growing out of my ear and I'd better get off. Hanging up the receiver, I looked at the sketches spread out on my bed. They really were good. Tad's artistic ability was nil, but he was right about exaggerating things to make them funnier. *How ironic*, I thought to myself. *Although he'd used different words, Tad had made the same criticism of my work that Mrs. Gibbons had.* People looked at my art and admired it, but never really felt personally involved. I pulled my portfolio out from under my bed. That night I'd go through every piece I'd done, to see how I could make it more appealing. An exercise like that would be good for me, and it might also help to keep my thoughts off the dance at school. I wondered who Tad was taking. No doubt she was pretty and very happy to be going with him. I wondered if Tad had found a florist who'd had time to make a corsage for him. I'd never gotten a corsage. In our little town in South Dakota, no one did things like that. The winter formal was the best dance of the Washington High School year, and I'd have liked to go.

I thought about my conversation with Sandy. Maybe Harold would have asked me to the dance if I'd been a bit more encouraging. He'd kind of hinted at it, but I hadn't wanted to seem too forward, and flirting was next to impossible for a shy person like me. *Well*, I told myself, pulling the first still life out of my portfolio, *even if I were there tonight with Harold, I might not even see Tad anyway. And if I did, he might not even remember about asking me to dance. Guys as popular as Tad Gordon probably dish out those kind of lines so often that they forget them as soon as they say them.*

Chapter Seven

Sunday afternoon went by much too quickly. Every time I thought about having to walk into Tad's house all by myself that evening, the clock hands seemed to jump ahead. By four o'clock I was seriously considering calling Sandy and telling her that she or Ellen—or better yet, both of them—just had to come with me. By five o'clock I'd talked myself out of that idea. First of all, it would be rude to bring them without asking Tad, and I certainly wasn't going to phone him. Second, I never knew what Sandy was going to say—and I wanted some control over what those kids might find out about me.

By five-thirty I was sure I was getting the flu. Much to my mother's displeasure, I told her that I couldn't eat a thing for dinner and then I went to my room to figure out what to wear. Everyone would probably be dressed fairly casually. My first choice was jeans, a button-down shirt, and a navy sweater vest. After putting them on, I cast a critical eye in the mirror and decided that I looked too preppy. I kept trying different things on, and by outfit number five, I was running out of clothes. My room looked as if a huge tornado had hit it. My mom would have died if she'd walked in right then. I knew I'd have to leave enough time to pick up at least some of the stuff off the floor.

"Honey," my dad called from downstairs, "if you want me to drop you off at that meeting on time, you'd better be ready in five minutes."

I stared into the mirror again. The black stirrup pants and red-and-black sweatshirt I was wearing looked as good or better than anything else I'd tried on. Besides, it had a bit more flair, and since I was supposed to be an artist, it might be good to look the part. I pulled all my hair over one shoulder and tied it with a red ribbon. *Well, that helps a little*, I thought, smiling at my reflection. *At least I look a little more grown-up.*

I started to put my clothes back in the closet, but my icy fingers could barely get them on the hangers. I rubbed my hands together, even though I knew that my nervousness was what was making them cold. Maybe it would be a good idea to get to Tad's a little late. Even though I'd have to meet everyone all at once, at least I wouldn't have to try to make small talk with one person while I waited for the others to arrive.

"Donna," my dad called, "come on. You said you were supposed to be there at seven, right? Besides, I want to be back for the beginning of my TV show. I'll wait for you in the car."

Well, I thought to myself, *so much for getting there fashionably late.* I walked into the living room and told my mom that I was ready. My father was still looking for his keys.

"Hey, you look beautiful!" he exclaimed when he saw me in the doorway.

"Thanks, Dad," I replied. It was sweet of him to say so, but he *was* my father. Too bad the whole world couldn't see me through his eyes!

I wished I could drive to Tad's myself, but I still had two more months to go until I got my license. The rest of the kids probably knew one another well, and I figured that many of them would arrive together. I just hoped no one would see my dad driving me to the party.

"You know," said my father as we got in the car, "Mom and I are so pleased to see you getting involved in the school here. I like that Tad Gordon, too. What do you think of him?"

I knew what my father was hinting at, but I said, "I think he has a good chance to be elected student-body president."

The next thing I knew I was standing all alone on the front walkway of Tad's house, holding my portfolio. Right then, I'd have been glad to change places with anyone.

Hesitantly I approached the front door. Unable to find a doorbell, I knocked on the door. No one answered, so I knocked harder. Tad *had* meant that night, hadn't he? My heart started to pound. Just then the front porch lights went on, and I finally saw the doorbell. I pushed it, and the door opened immediately.

"Well, hi," said Tad, looking sheepish. "Sorry, I thought someone had already turned on the front lights. Come on in. Some more kids are coming later, but I'll introduce you to the ones who are here." *So*, I thought as we walked into a large family room, *I wasn't the first or the last person to arrive after all.* I took that as a good omen.

About five kids were sitting on the floor munching popcorn and talking and laughing. "Hey, guys, listen up!" Tad said. They turned toward him expectantly. "This is Donna Newbury, and wait until you see what she's got for our campaign." No sooner had he spoken than the doorbell rang again, and Tad went to get it.

Leaning my portfolio against the sofa, I went to sit down with the group on the floor. I didn't know any of their names, but a girl I recognized as one of the cheerleaders said, "Hi, I'm Angie. You look familiar. Didn't you work on Tad's campaign last year?"

"No, I didn't," I said, hoping my nervousness wouldn't be too obvious. "I just moved to Tucson this year."

"Oh, that must have been really hard. I'd die if I ever had to leave Washington High. It's such a great school." I had the feeling Angie might do a cheer on the spot. "So, how do you know Tad?" she asked.

I took a deep breath. What was I going to say? That I didn't really know him at all? That I'd accosted him in the lunchroom because I needed a way to get my art grade raised? Fortunately, before I could answer, Tad's latest guest entered the family room.

His name was Andy, and everyone seemed happy to see him. I was quickly forgotten, so I sat back and relaxed a bit.

As the conversation swirled about me, I realized that it wasn't really so different from the things that Ellen and Sandy and I discussed. Even these popular kids talked about tests, clothes, and who was going out with whom. For the most part, they seemed to know one another pretty well, and from the sound of things, they'd worked on a lot of these campaigns together.

After I'd been at the party about twenty minutes, I began to feel practically invisible. I'd barely seen Tad, and I wondered if this meeting was just going to be kids putting music on the stereo and sitting around talking. Then another girl walked in with Tad. She had the most perfectly shaped almond eyes I'd ever seen, and her jet-black hair was cut into a short, sophisticated style. She wore a rose-colored sweater, and her long, well-manicured nails rested lightly on Tad's arm.

"Well, I guess that's about everyone," Tad said, shutting the family-room doors. "OK, you guys," he began. "Let's get this meeting going. Friday night was the traditional kick-off blast, but tonight is the official start of another Gordon campaign." He threw himself onto the couch and put his feet up on the coffee table.

Someone groaned. "So how many does this make, Tad?"

"Hey, look on the bright side," Tad said, laughing. "This is positively the last one we'll ever be involved in at Washington."

The girl with the almond eyes was sitting right next to Tad. She leaned closer to him and said, "It's too bad that there has to be an election at all. You deserve to finish out your senior year as student-body president. Christy should've kept her promise."

An uneasy silence fell over the room. Obviously there was something about this whole thing with Christy that I didn't know. What was it that Tad had said about her when he was at my house? "Well," said Tad, with what seemed like forced cheerfulness, "we'd have missed having one last campaign battle and all the parties that go with it. Besides, we've got a secret weapon this time around." He looked at me. "Donna, that's your cue!"

My eyes grew wide. "Well," I started. My mind was blank. What would I say in front of all these people? "I'll get the pictures," I told Tad, "and you explain, OK?"

The girl with the almond eyes looked sulky

as Tad came to stand next to me. "Here, I'll help you get those out," he said, reaching for my portfolio. "Ladies and gentlemen, meet Tad the Terrific and his mighty mascot, the Washington Warrior."

"They're great, Tad!" Andy exclaimed. "You never looked so good!" Other favorable comments flooded the room, and I was bursting with pride. They loved my artwork! I *was* someone special.

Tad held up a hand in protest. "Hey, guys, I'm not taking any of the credit here. These are all Donna's creations. She and I worked together all day yesterday, and this is what we came up with. Every day she's going to draw a huge new comic strip to post outside the library. Think that will get people's attention?" Tad looked at me and winked, and although I tried not to, I blushed a little. If this was what it was like to be in the limelight, it really wasn't bad at all.

"Hey, Elaine," Andy said, nudging the girl with the almond eyes, "don't you think Tad looks a lot better in these pictures than he did all dressed up for the dance last night?"

My mind immediately registered the significance of his words. So, *she'd* been the one he'd had to get a corsage for. Well, what had I expected? Elaine was pretty, sophisticated, and very self-assured. *It doesn't matter*, I told myself. *You're only here to do art for the campaign. There's no point in letting yourself get lulled into thinking you're part of Tad Gordon's life in any other way!*

Tad left the room to get another big bowl of popcorn, and when he returned, the group turned its attention to the comic-strip story line. They wanted to put up a new installment every day, building the story to a climax right before election.

"I've got it," said a tall boy, who I thought was one of the basketball players. "For the final episode the day before the voting, we could put on a skit. You know, bring the comic strip to life. If Gordon really hammed up Tad the Terrific, he'd be a shoo-in. Everyone will think it's hysterical."

Story-line ideas, as well as a lot of cracks and comments, flew back and forth. Most of the ideas were absurd and totally unusable, but everyone was having a great time. I found myself laughing at other people's jokes without feeling self-conscious about not saying much myself. To my great surprise, when I glanced at my watch later I found that it was almost ten o'clock. We still hadn't worked out all of the plots, but we had enough material for the first couple of episodes. Three kids volunteered to get together with Tad and write the rest of the strips. We'd really need them by the end of the week because the same kids had said that they'd color in my drawings.

At ten-thirty the meeting began to break up. "I've still got to study for one of Rosen's tests tonight," said Andy. "Anybody need a ride?" Several people took him up on his offer. And soon almost everyone had left. While I didn't feel nearly so uncomfortable as I had when I'd arrived, I still felt funny about asking any of the kids to take me home. Waiting until Tad was almost alone, I asked him if I could use the phone. "Do you need a ride?" he asked.

"Oh, that's OK," I said. "I really didn't want to bother anyone, and I wasn't sure anyone lived that close to me."

"Hey, no problem." He smiled at me, and a lock of his thick, wavy hair fell over his forehead. "I can run you home."

"But—"

Tad cut me off. "Donna, if I didn't want to do it, I wouldn't offer. We'll just wait until the last person clears out of here. OK?"

"OK," I agreed, trying not to look too pleased.

We stood in the hallway for a few minutes, talking. I couldn't believe how much easier it was now to have a conversation with Tad. He offered to bring some paper over to my house the next day, and I felt a warm glow flood my body.

Tad was just telling me again how pleased everyone was with my cartoon, when Elaine came up behind us.

"Oh, there you guys are," she said, looking at me accusingly. "We didn't know what had happened to you two. Tad, a few people still have questions for you about the campaign."

I could feel myself beginning to blush, but Tad replied, "I'll bet you could answer them all, Elaine. How many years have we done these campaigns together, anyway?"

Elaine smiled, but she offered no answer. I didn't know if Tad noticed, but I felt her eyes fixed icily on me. "I, uh, Tad was going to give me a ride home," I said, feeling compelled to explain. "As soon as everyone leaves, I mean."

Elaine's voice dripped sweetness. "Well, that's no problem, Donna. I'll drop you off, and we can let Tad relax. He's got a lot of planning to do, and besides, everyone may not leave for a while. You wouldn't want to hurry them out or anything, right?"

Suddenly I felt about two years old. "Well, OK. Thanks," I said meekly. We said goodbye to Tad and walked out to Elaine's car. "This is a beautiful car," I said, sliding into the passenger seat.

"Thanks." She smiled a toothpaste-perfect smile. "So, where do you live?"

I told her, and she took off down the road. We talked all the way to my house, and Elaine seemed nice enough. I began to wonder if I'd been imagining that she'd resented me earlier. After all, taking me home was out of her way. She was probably just trying to save Tad a trip and being nice to me. Feeling guilty, I thanked her profusely when we arrived at my house.

"Donna," she began hesitantly, shutting off the ignition, "maybe I'm butting in where I shouldn't, but if you're going to be part of our group for the next few weeks, you might as well know."

"Know what?" I asked, perplexed.

"That Tad is the world's biggest flirt. You don't want to get taken in by all the stuff he says. I've known him a long time, and I've seen a lot of girls get hurt." She smiled sympathetically. "Oh, by the way, I really think your artwork is super."

I wasn't sure what to say. In fact, I wasn't quite sure what Elaine was talking about or why she'd made a point of saying anything at all. I half mumbled my thanks again and got out of the car. Elaine started the engine and roared off. I went in our front door, feeling totally exhausted and extremely confused.

Chapter Eight

When I got to my room, the clothes I hadn't had time to clean up before I'd left were still waiting for me, along with a note from my mother that let me know she'd seen the mess. *Good thing she didn't see this room at its worst,* I thought, picking up the rest of my clothes.

As I put things away, I tried to sort everything out in my mind. I felt a little like Alice in Wonderland—everything just kept getting curiouser and curiouser, and nothing was turning out the way I'd thought it would. I'd been really scared to meet Tad's friends, but they'd turned out to be nice enough. I'd been petrified that they might think my caricatures were stupid, but everyone had liked them a lot. And then, there was Tad. A few times I'd been sure that Tad thought I was someone special, but then it seemed as if he made everyone feel important in some way. Maybe that was why he was popular and won so many elections. And what had been the problem with Christy, anyway? Maybe Sandy would know. I got ready for bed, promising myself that I'd ask her the next day. But before I fell asleep, I had to admit that the most confusing part of the evening had been Elaine. I didn't know why I felt the way I did about her. She'd gone out of her way to be nice, but I wasn't sure she could be trusted. Yawning, I asked myself if the reason I didn't like Elaine was because Andy had implied that Tad was going out with her.

Soon I was fast asleep, and before I knew it, my alarm clock was blaring the beginning of another Monday morning. I dressed for school very carefully and left the house without breakfast.

I didn't get a chance to see Sandy until noon. As soon as we had piled our trays with what the cafeteria called food, I asked her what she knew about the rivalry between Christy and Tad.

"Not too much," Sandy replied, taking a bite of her pizza.

"Well, did they ever run against each other before?" I asked, trying to prod her memory.

"Let's see," she said, crunching the ice in her soda. "I think they ran against each other their freshman year. Of course, I was still in junior high, so I don't know that much about it. I'm not sure who won, but somehow, I think it was Christy. Then, my freshman year, Tad was sophomore-class president."

Ellen set her tray down and joined us. "Boy, the line for Mexican food was so long that I didn't think I was ever going to get through it. Lunch is practically over." Her enchiladas looked pretty soggy, but I didn't say anything. "Hey," she said to me, "how'd it go last night?"

"Fine. We were just talking about the class elections for the last few years. Do you know if there's some sort of special rivalry between Christy and Tad?"

Ellen chuckled as she dug her fork into her horrible-looking lunch. "Boy, that's putting it mildly. I mean, ordinarily I wouldn't know about stuff like that, but my older brother is just a year older than they are. I remember him coming home and talking about the class elections. Christy beat Tad by only two votes out of the entire freshman class. Then, at the end of his freshman year, Tad ran against her for sophomore-class president. He won, but it was pretty close that time, too. I don't know for sure, but I've heard that they made some kind of deal their junior year. Tad agreed not to run for president, and he even helped Christy's campaign. In return, she promised not to run against him for student-body president this semester." Ellen paused for a moment to take a swig of her chocolate milk. "Of course, I don't know if all that's true, because Christy's certainly running against him. Everyone says the two of them have dated off and on all through high school. Geez, talk about love not running smoothly!"

That was one of the longest speeches I'd ever heard Ellen make. I could tell by the look on Sandy's face that she wasn't too thrilled about being scooped. "Well, I guess your brother must know." She shrugged. "What's with all this ancient history anyway, Donna? You haven't even told us about last night."

Poking at my inedible hamburger, I told them that my cartoons had been a big hit. "I just hope that they'll still work when they're five times the size of my sketches."

The lunch bell rang much sooner than we expected, and we headed toward our next classes. The afternoon dragged, until I was sure that it would never end. Walking out of my last-period class, I heard a familiar voice behind me.

"Hi! Are you ready to go to work?"

Smiling, I turned around. I hadn't thought it was possible for Tad's eyes to be any bluer, but the sweater he was wearing made them even more attractive than before.

"How'd you know where my last class was?" I asked in surprise.

Tad grinned. "Hey, there are some benefits to being a senior around here. Listen, I'd love some help picking out the paper for the cartoons. If you're free, I'll give you a ride home after we stop at the store."

Flustered, I blurted out, "But all you need is butcher paper. I thought last night you said you were just going to buy a roll of it."

Now it was Tad's turn to look a little bit embarrassed. "Well, that's right. I guess I did. So you caught on to me, huh? I'll tell you what. Why don't you come with me to pick up the butcher paper, and then we could stop at Swensen's for a soda. We could start on the cartoons afterward, if you want."

My heart leaped with joy. Tad didn't need me to go with him to get butcher paper. And he certainly didn't have to take me out for a soda unless he wanted to. That thought was far sweeter than any soda. It was almost impossible to believe, but Tad Gordon might actually be interested in *me*!

Part of me was all ready to say no because I was afraid I'd say or do something wrong, but I knew I couldn't give up a chance like this. "That'd be nice," I responded with a smile.

"Great. I've got to ditch some of these books in my locker, so I'll meet you in the parking lot, OK?"

As soon as Tad was out of sight, I ran to the nearest girls' room and dug through my purse to find my comb and lipstick. I pulled the comb through my hair quickly, hitting a few tangles and wincing as I yanked through them. I wished I had some blusher with me, but after another check of my purse, I was sure I'd left most of my makeup at home. The lipstick would have to do.

The mirrors in the girls' room weren't much, but I stood on my tiptoes and tried to make sure that my blouse was tucked into my skirt. Everything looked OK. I leaned toward the mirror a bit, and my blue eyes stared back at me. Elaine's eyes hinted of mystery, but mine were the kind that made people pinch my cheek or pat me on the head.

Come on, I told myself. *There is absolutely nothing more you can do about the way you look right now, so quit stalling and get moving!*

I was almost out the front door of the school when I heard someone call my name. I turned to see Elaine hurrying toward me. "Donna, wait up!" she called. "You look as if you're running to a fire. Where are you going in such a rush?"

I stopped. "I, uh, was just meeting Tad to get some things for the campaign. You know, art supplies and all."

"Really." Elaine looked surprised. "Well, maybe I can help you two."

Remembering how nice she'd been to take me home the night before, I felt compelled to say that that would be a great idea. My heart sank as Elaine fell into step with me on the way to Tad's car. What else could I have done? I asked myself. There was no reason to lie to her, and she was Tad's girlfriend, after all.

As we reached the car, Tad looked at the two of us, bewildered. I planned to explain why Elaine was with me, but before I could say a word, Elaine began. "Hi, Tad! Hope I'm not butting in on anything, but Donna really wanted me to join you guys. I'll be glad to help, really."

I was ashamed of myself, but I wished I hadn't invited her to come with us at all. I'd only done it to be polite. Mentally, I crossed my fingers that Tad would tell Elaine this was just a project for him and me, but he opened the passenger door without a word and went around to the driver's side. When we started off, I found myself in the backseat, and Elaine was sitting up front next to Tad. How had things worked out that way?

The day turned into even more of a fiasco later, if that was possible. After we'd gotten the butcher paper, Tad asked for a rain check on the soda. He told us he'd just remembered telling Andy that he'd help him with his geometry. "Look, why don't I drop you two off at Donna's, and you can get started with the drawing and coloring."

I wasn't too thrilled with that idea. Elaine made me very nervous, and besides, I needed to sketch the entire cartoon out first to make sure it would work. I wouldn't be ready for anyone to color for quite a while. I told Tad that I really wasn't ready for any help yet, and Elaine said that was just as well because she really needed to get home. She'd gladly help another day, she assured us.

The next thing I knew, I'd been let off in front of my house with a large roll of butcher paper, and Elaine and Tad were roaring off into the sunset. I felt like crying as they left.

It doesn't matter, I told myself. *It's the art that matters.* But somehow, that well-worn phrase was beginning to sound more hollow every time I said it. The art was important, of course, but I'd started dreaming about being with Tad and having him think of me as a girl, instead of just as someone who drew well.

I lugged the paper into the house and unrolled a seven-foot section. If there were going to be three cartoon panels . . . I took out a ruler and began measuring to see how large everything would actually have to be.

Three hours later I'd finished drawing my first cartoon. On such a large scale, it had been much harder to get the proportions right than I'd anticipated. There were lots of extra pencil lines, so I got out my paints and began to add some color. I was anxious to see what the finished panel would look like.

My parents had gone out for dinner with one of my dad's business clients, and I was glad. No one made me stop to eat dinner, and I told my growling stomach it would just have to wait until my work was done. Finally I put the last touch of blue paint on Tad's eyes, and the first cartoon was officially done.

My back ached from leaning over so much, but the results were terrific. The small sketch I'd shown everyone at the meeting the night before was nothing compared to the way the characters looked after being reproduced on four-foot-high butcher paper. Tad the Terrific stood toweringly tall on skinny legs, which were emphasized by the oversize shorts I had him wearing. His huge feet were clad in high-top basketball shoes, and the Washington colors, green and white, flowed on a cape that would easily rival Superman's. Of course, Tad's had a big *T* on it instead of an *S*. I hadn't been able to bring myself to ruin Tad's perfect features by making them cartoonlike. Instead, I'd made his jaw a little more prominent and his eyes so vividly blue that they seemed to jump right out of the picture.

I stood back and admired my work. I couldn't believe I'd actually done a successful cartoon, and I could hardly wait for Tad to see it.

Sheer enthusiasm carried me to the phone to dial Tad's number. I'd never have had the nerve if I'd stopped to think about what I was doing. The phone rang twice before a woman answered it. "I'm sorry, he's not home," she said. "This is Tad's mother. Can I take a message?"

A wave of disappointment swept over me, and I wished I could just hang up. "Uh, could you tell him that Donna finished the first cartoon for his campaign?" Mrs. Gordon said she would, and I thanked her and said good-bye.

Suddenly I felt exhausted. How could I be so tired? Glancing at the clock, I saw to my amazement that it was almost nine-thirty. I'd been working on that thing for over five hours. Considering that I'd promised to have a new cartoon ready every day for ten days . . . I groaned and covered my eyes. I didn't even want to *think* about how long it was going to take me to do all of that work. My other grades were going to be completely down the tubes by the time Tad's campaign was over.

Walking into the kitchen, I took a piece of leftover pizza from the refrigerator and stuck it in the oven to reheat. As I waited for it to be ready, I couldn't help wondering if Tad was at Elaine's. Maybe they'd dropped me off and gone to her house. He was probably still there. If I could have been sure he was with her, I'd just call Elaine's, and then both of them could come over and see the cartoon. That made perfect sense, but somehow, I couldn't force myself to pick up the phone again.

While I'd been thinking, the pizza had burned. I took the smoking slice from the oven and dumped it in the garbage. *Great*, I thought. *I'm starved, and now I've ruined dinner.* My mood was becoming fouler by the minute, and my back was really beginning to hurt.

Just then the phone rang, startling me. *Sandy,* I thought, but I was too pooped to talk. I looked at the phone, willing it to stop ringing, but it didn't. "Hello," I answered, annoyed.

"Donna, it's Tad. I just got your message. You're incredible! If it's not too late for company, I'd love to come over and see the cartoon."

"No, I mean, yes." At least Tad couldn't see me blushing over the phone wires. "No, it's not too late, and, yes, by all means, come over."

"I'm on my way," he said.

Hanging up the phone, I no longer felt the least bit tired. I tore into my room and shuddered as I looked in the mirror. Tad would arrive soon, and I was an absolute mess. My mascara had run from rubbing my eyes while I worked. My clothes were grubby and wrinkled, and at most I'd have ten minutes to pull myself back together. It wouldn't be an easy task, but the sparkle in my eyes said it was definitely going to be worthwhile!

Chapter Nine

Shoving my hair into my mom's big shower cap, I jumped into an icy shower. There was no time to wait for the water to heat, and I shivered as the cold spray hit my body. In two minutes flat, I was out of the shower and dumping scented powder over myself. My hands were shaking, and not just from the cold. If only my parents were home. Then they'd be able to get the door, and I could at least have a little more time to get ready. Quickly I put on the new purple shirt I'd been saving for a special occasion and paired it with black cords. The doorbell rang just as I finished reapplying my makeup.

I grabbed my favorite cologne and sprayed it on my wrists. *It can't hurt,* I thought, putting down the bottle and heading for the front door. Taking a deep breath, I tried to open it casually, as if I always got visits from gorgeous guys.

"Hi, Donna," Tad said warmly as he stepped inside. "So, lead me to it. I'm dying to see the poster."

I took him into the family room to see the finished cartoon. For a minute he didn't say anything at all, and I was afraid that maybe he wouldn't think it was so great after all. "Did anyone help you with this?" he asked finally. "I mean, it's great, but it looks like it must have taken you hours."

"Well, no," I said, nervously twirling a piece of my hair. "I sort of started it myself when you dropped me off after school today."

Tad shook his head and ran a hand through his wavy hair. "Donna, this is absolutely the most incredible thing I've ever seen. I can't believe you did the whole cartoon in one day. It's terrific. But I don't want you working this hard in the future. From now on, we're getting you some help. If it weren't so late already, I'd take you out for a soda, or something, to at least say thanks."

Part of me wanted to say it wasn't too late, and I'd go out with him then, but it was almost ten-fifteen. My parents would be furious if I went anywhere. "I'll have to take a rain check," I said softly. "My folks would worry if I went out. But you could have a soda right here if you want."

Tad's deep voice sounded sincere as he told me he'd like that a lot. For the next half hour we sat sipping our sodas and talking. At first I was really nervous, but I got so interested in what he was saying about the election that I forgot all about being self-conscious and just listened.

"I guess I'd really like to win because I always thought I'd finish high school as student-body president," Tad began. He bit his lip. "That sounds kind of conceited, huh? I didn't mean it to. I'm also hoping to get a scholarship to Arizona State. I thought being president might make my high school record look better." Tad sighed, and a frown creased his brow. "And then, of course, to be perfectly honest, there's the whole mess with Christy. I'd be lying if I said I didn't want to beat her." For a moment he seemed lost in his own thoughts, and more to himself than to me, he added, "What she did last year was pretty rotten."

I was dying to know exactly what she had done, but it seemed rude to ask. I had a feeling it was the same story that Ellen had told me and Sandy. Besides, I didn't want to interrupt Tad. I could sit next to him like that and listen to him talk forever.

Just then the door opened, and my parents walked in. I glanced at my watch and saw that it was almost eleven. My father saw Tad and didn't say anything, but I noticed him lift one eyebrow in amusement. "Hi, Mom. Hi, Dad," I said quickly. "You remember Tad, don't you? I just finished his first cartoon, and he came over to have a look at it. Come see!"

My parents walked into the family room to look at the huge poster, which took up much of the floor. It was exciting to watch the expressions on their faces turn from amazement to pride. Tad noticed, too, and he said enthusiastically, "This is going to be the talk of the school. By the time the election rolls around, the student body may write in Donna for president." Tad must have had a lot of experience with girls' parents because he immediately added, "Sorry it got so late. I guess we lost track of the time."

I could see that my mother was impressed by Tad's politeness. "Oh, that's all right," she said. "Donna, why don't you walk Tad to the door? Tad, good luck. We hope you win."

Walking Tad out, I felt some of my shyness return, but before he left, he took both my hands in his. "Donna, I don't even know how to thank you. But from now on, you're not working this hard alone. We'll all help you paint. I, for one, will enjoy working by your side. Good night, Donna." He leaned over and kissed me on the cheek, and I honestly thought I would melt right there on the spot.

I was sure that was the most perfect moment of my life, but things got even better the next day. Tad came over at lunch and sat right down at our table. "Mind if I join you?" he asked. I thought Sandy was going to swallow her apple whole. He took out a piece of paper, and together we planned a schedule of when and where the sign-making meetings would take place. After Tad had left, there was an awed silence at the table.

"And to think," said Sandy finally, "that I used to be the one encouraging you to talk to boys. Maybe you just never found the right one to talk to before."

Ellen looked a little forlorn. "Well, I guess we won't be seeing much of you until after the election, Donna."

"Not true," I said loyally. "You're my best friends, and you're certainly welcome to come to any of the meetings at my house!" I really wasn't sure, though, if that was OK or not. I still remembered how Christy had snubbed me when I'd wanted to help with her campaign. I knew that I wasn't exactly a member of Tad's crowd, but I didn't care. Sandy and Ellen were my best friends, and it was my house, so they could come, too.

We began meeting almost every night to work on Tad's campaign. One evening, when Elaine had arrived before everyone else, we started talking. "I sure hope Tad beats Christy," she said. "It would serve her right."

It was too perfect a cue to pass up. "What happened last year?" I asked.

"Oh, I forgot you were new this year," Elaine said. "Well, first of all, no matter who else runs for office, Tad or Christy always wins. Last year the two of them started dating. I think Tad was pretty crazy about her. Anyway, they decided it wouldn't do much for their relationship to be campaigning against each other, so they talked it over and decided that if Tad skipped running for junior-class president, Christy wouldn't run for student-body president their senior year."

"But," I interrupted, "since there are now elections both semesters why didn't one of them run the first semester and the other run the second? Then they both could have been elected."

Elaine looked at me as if I were from outer space. "The first-semester people don't get to *do* anything. It's the second semester that's the best time to be a class officer at Washington. That's when all the big events are." She tapped one of her perfect fingernails on the table. "Anyway, getting back to the campaign between Christy and Tad, he didn't run last year as they'd agreed. In fact, he helped with Christy's campaign, and she won easily. Then this year Christy and Tad went from being steadies to having an occasional date, and I guess she went to him a few weeks ago and said she'd always wanted to run for student-body president. She said she didn't blame him for being mad, but she'd only have one shot at it, and if she didn't try, she'd never forgive herself."

By this time several other kids had wandered into the room, and Elaine turned to them. I sat thinking about what she had said. As I drew cartoons that night, I hoped that somehow my posters might help Tad get the victory he deserved.

A week later the first poster went up. I'd been so nervous the night before that I'd tossed and turned the whole night. But all my worrying seemed to be for nothing. The reactions to my cartoon were every bit as positive as Tad had predicted.

Everyone who was working on Tad's campaign went to a party at his house that night to celebrate. In the middle of the evening, someone put on some music, and a few couples started dancing. Soon more kids had joined them, and Sandy started dancing with Andy. Tad hadn't minded her coming at all. *They'd make a good couple,* I thought happily. I also noticed that Elaine had taken Tad's hand and dragged him out to dance. Much as I hated to admit it, they moved well together—as if they'd had lots of practice.

Then someone turned the lights down and put a slow song on the stereo. My eyes were still adjusting to the darkened room when a familiar voice said, "Hey, there you are! I've been looking all over for you. Want to dance?"

Tad's arms encircled my waist. As we moved to the music, I thought that this was even better than it had been in my dream. Though I hadn't had a lot of practice, Tad was easy to follow, and we danced without speaking for two or three songs. Then the lights suddenly went on again. "Hey, guys," came Elaine's voice. "One triumphant beginning does not make a winning campaign. We'd better get some work done tonight." There were a few groans, but in a matter of minutes the paints and paper had been brought to the middle of the room. A few of the partygoers suddenly remembered they had homework to do, but most of the group stayed on and got to work.

The next morning, kids were gathered around the library wall, waiting for the new cartoon to go up. The previous day's had introduced the characters, and that day the story line would begin. As I watched Tad take down my first cartoon, I felt a pang of sadness. So much work for just one day. But it was great to see how everyone eagerly crowded around the wall, laughing at the new installment.

Even Mrs. Gibbon's mentioned my poster. Right after the bell rang, she said, "I see that one of the artists in this class is proving my oft-stated philosophy that art can instill all kinds of feelings in others." I thought about how my new view of art was affecting me personally. I was excited to have other people appreciate my work. At one time that would have been all that mattered, but now there was the added joy of having suddenly become a minor celebrity at school. Then, of course, there was the unexpected thrill of having a king-size crush on Tad Gordon and deep, deep down, believing that he might be interested in me, too. I hadn't told that to anyone, and I didn't intend to. Tad was being so nice to me, and even if he'd only asked me to dance the night before out of politeness, he certainly hadn't had to keep paying all that attention to me. Now I almost felt like going up to Mrs. Gibbons and hugging her. Not only was her project improving my art technique, but my whole life as well.

That night Elaine, Sandy, Tad, and I were putting the finishing details on a new poster. Elaine and Sandy were at the other end of the roll, painting and arguing about which one of them was more stubborn. "So," Tad said to me casually, "what would you think about dinner and a movie Saturday night?"

I was so amazed that I blurted out, "With me?"

Tad laughed, "Well, yes. I thought you and I could go together, like on a date."

Blushing, I said, "That'd be nice," and hoped that I didn't sound too ecstatic. I wished I could run over to Sandy and tell her Tad had actually asked me out, but I guessed she had overheard. When she caught my eye, she winked.

Wednesday was also glorious with everything continuing perfectly. Then on Thursday, midway through the afternoon, I passed the library and noticed that a part of my poster had been ripped. It was stupid, I guess, but I felt almost as if part of me had been torn. I went into the library and borrowed some tape to fix the tear. *Maybe it was an accident*, I told myself.

All day I felt slightly uneasy. Later, at our sign painting, I mentioned the damaged poster, but no one seemed overly concerned. Even Tad just shrugged. They were right. There were so many kids passing by the library every day that there were bound to be some mishaps. The object of the cartoons was to get attention, and we had certainly done that. Even some of the teachers were saying that Tad's campaign was about the cleverest they'd seen. Christy and her friends were walking around with worried frowns on their faces. They were using Care Bears on their posters and were trying to make them convey the idea of caring about the school. The idea was cute, and the posters looked nice, but no one paid much attention to them.

Friday morning Tad and Andy arrived at school early to put up the latest episode of our cartoon story. It had gotten so crowded around the library by first bell that they could barely fight their way through to the wall.

I, on the other hand, got to school twenty

minutes late. Keeping up with my school-work, drawing all those huge posters, and thinking about Tad were taking their toll on me. I'd been too exhausted to move that morning. My mom had agreed that as long as I didn't make a habit of being tardy, I could sleep late one time.

After arriving at school, I checked in at the attendance office and then headed toward my history class. Figuring it couldn't hurt to stop and see the latest cartoon in place, I passed by the library. But when I looked up at my poster, I gasped.

The cartoon was ruined, and this time it couldn't have been an accident. Someone had taken a black felt-tip marker and scribbled all across the figures. It was a total mess. Some of the words were no longer readable. I fought back the tears. It wasn't fair! After all that work, someone had deliberately trashed the poster before most people had even gotten to look at it.

Chapter Ten

Tad had been so angry when he saw the ruined poster that he went storming to Mr. Lunder, the student-council sponsor, and dragged him to see the damage. From the look on the teacher's face, we could tell he was disgusted with the vandalism.

One of Tad's friends shouted, "Christy should be disqualified!" A few other kids in the crowd that had followed them agreed with him.

Mr. Lunder was silent at first and then he said that he didn't think anyone should jump to conclusions. There was no proof that Christy had done anything, he pointed out. And while he agreed that the destruction of student property shouldn't be tolerated, he didn't believe in making hasty accusations.

110

"I'll work on getting to the bottom of this situation," he had assured us. Meanwhile, he wanted to see both Christy and Tad in his office after school.

The ruined poster was the talk of the school for the rest of the day. Sandy, Ellen, and I eavesdropped on the table next to us at lunch. Most of the kids had decided that Christy or some of her friends were responsible for the vandalism. A few disagreed, saying that it was probably the same kids who went around spraying graffiti on lockers and plugging keyholes with glue. One boy was sure that Tad had done it himself. "After all," he pointed out, "it gets him a lot of attention, right? And besides, everyone feels sorry for poor Tad that way. It's a great campaign tactic."

We weren't having a meeting that Friday night, but I'd hoped that Tad would call and let me know what Mr. Lunder had said. I kept wondering if Christy had confessed to ruining our poster. By nine that evening it was clear that Tad wasn't going to call. I didn't want to phone him since we had a date for the next night. My curiosity was killing me, but I'd just have to wait until Saturday to find out what had happened.

Sandy came over the next day, and the two of us went through my closet, trying to figure out what I should wear to a movie and dinner. I really wanted to look good for Tad, and I was very nervous. "I mean, what if we get away from all this art and campaign stuff, and he decides he doesn't like me at all?" I moaned.

Sandy shook her head. "Every time I think there's hope for you and you're beginning to sound a bit more confident, you say something that makes me think we're getting nowhere. Donna, Tad could take out any girl at Washington High. We all know how badly Elaine wants him, but he asked *you* out. So quit worrying about everything, and just have a good time."

I laughed nervously. "That's easy for you to say. You aren't the one who's going to make a total fool of herself."

Sandy heaved an exaggerated sigh. "I wouldn't mind if I were." She sighed again. "Actually, I wish Andy would ask me out. I'd love to go to the Victory Dance with him."

"What's that?" I asked.

"Oops," Sandy said. "I forgot. Another of dear old Washington's traditions that you haven't been here long enough to know about. The election results are announced at a dance that night at school. After that, the new student-body president stands up and gives

112

a thank-you speech. You don't have to have a date or anything. Some kids go alone, but it's lots more fun if you go with someone. Just think, you'll probably have the new student-body president by your side."

"Oh, I don't think so—"

Sandy started to giggle. "Boy, we're really something. A month ago those senior boys didn't even know we existed, and we were scared to death to talk to them. It's amazing how things change, huh? And I *do* think Tad'll ask you to the Victory Dance. He might even ask you tonight. For crying out loud, Donna, the way the guy's been watching your every move means he's not *only* interested in you as an artist."

There was no point in arguing with Sandy. Once she'd made up her mind about something, that was it. Besides, I had to admit that, secretly, I hoped she was right.

As we talked, I tried on just about everything I owned. Nothing in my closet met with Sandy's approval, so it was on to her house and her own bedroom closet. I ended up borrowing her new green sweater dress. With a navy belt slung over one hip, I thought I looked really terrific. Well, maybe that was a slight exaggeration, but at least I didn't look like I was twelve years old.

113

After I'd finally left Sandy's, I didn't have that much time to get ready. It seemed like no time at all until the doorbell rang. When Tad arrived, I could see the admiration in his eyes. "Wow," he said, "you look great!"

"Thanks," I replied. Then, trying to sound more like Elaine and the other popular girls, I added, "You look nice yourself."

We didn't say very much on the way to the theater. We'd decided to have dinner after the movie, since the lines would be shorter that way. By the time we finally found a parking space, the movie was about to begin. Once Tad had helped me out of the car, he kept my hand in his as we hurried toward the theater. We slid into our seats just as the opening credits began to roll. Tad leaned over and whispered, "Pretty good timing, huh?"

The movie was funny, and I enjoyed it almost as much as I enjoyed hearing Tad's rich laughter. Afterward, we went to Munchies for pizza, and we continued to talk and laugh about some of the best scenes. Midway through dinner I realized that we'd been together all that time and hadn't even mentioned the campaign. I could almost hear Sandy saying triumphantly, "See, I told you so." Still, I was really curious about what had happened at Tad's meeting with Mr. Lunder. And, maybe, if I brought that up, Tad would remember the Victory Dance. And then maybe . . .

"Hey," Tad said, breaking into my daydream. "What's the good news? Why are you smiling?" His relentless blue eyes looked inquisitively into mine.

"Oh, it's nothing," I replied. "So, what happened at your meeting with Mr. Lunder?"

Tad grimaced. "Nothing much, really. He made us promise to be good sports and campaign fairly."

"Then Christy didn't admit to wrecking our posters?"

"No," Tad sighed. "And I feel really terrible that I even suspected her. I should have known that she had too much class for that. Mr. Lunder said that one of the teachers had overheard Bob Smolington bragging to his friends that he was the one who ripped up our posters and that he was proud of it."

"You're kidding," I gasped. "Why? Who is Bob Smolington?"

"He's this real jerk in my class," Tad replied. "I don't think he cares a bit who wins the election. He just likes to cause trouble. His idea of fun is anything that messes up the system." Tad smiled at me tenderly. "Donna, I'm so sorry. I know how hard you worked on those cartoons and how important they are to you."

I felt like saying that the ruined posters weren't nearly so important to me as he was, but I didn't. Instead I told Tad that there'd be a new one up on Monday, and the whole thing would be forgotten.

Having finished the last slice of pizza, we headed to the car and drove home in silence. I didn't know quite what was wrong, but I felt decidedly uneasy. Had I said something wrong? When we reached my house, Tad turned off the motor. "Well, thanks," I said in what I hoped was a cheery voice. "I had a really good time."

"So did I," Tad replied quietly. He drummed his fingers on the steering wheel for a minute. Then, turning toward me, he asked, "Donna, how many hours do you think you've put in so far on my campaign?"

"Oh, I don't know," I said. "Lots. Why?"

"Just wondering, I guess." There was a strained sort of silence, as if neither of us knew what to say next. "Why? Why did you spend so much time on this?"

Stalling for time, I picked an imaginary piece of lint off my coat. This definitely wasn't the time to explain that I'd chosen him only because I needed the art grade and because Christy had rejected my offer of help. Besides, I was working on Tad's campaign for other reasons now. "Tad," I replied, forcing a smile, "why are you asking me all these questions? I've been helping you because I want you to win."

"Why?" He looked so vulnerable all of a sudden.

"Because I really—" His expression had almost made me blurt out that I was helping him because I really liked him, but I quickly reminded myself that I was talking to one of the most popular guys at school. Luckily I caught myself in time to keep from sounding like a little kid with a crush. Remembering the saying that a good offense was the best defense, I teased, "Why did you agree to let me help you?"

"Because you're a terrific artist." Tad's words popped out immediately, but then he sighed and banged his hand on the dashboard. "Donna, this is getting us nowhere. You sure don't make it easy for a guy to figure you out. OK, I'll be honest. Somebody has to start. Sure, I liked your art, but to tell you the truth, I'd made up my mind I wanted you to help on my campaign before I'd ever seen your poster."

"You did?" I gasped.

"Uh-huh. As we were walking to the Spanish room to get your folder, I was thinking that I'd like to get to know you."

"You were?" I couldn't believe what I was hearing. "Oh, Tad, that's so sweet!"

"And?" he questioned.

"And what?" I asked, floating in blissful confusion. I didn't know exactly where this conversation was going, but what had been said so far was perfectly OK with me.

"Well, what did you think about *me*? I mean, when I first met you, I'll admit I was conceited enough to think the art was just a ploy, that it was me you were interested in. Then I saw how you dug into your work, and I began to think that I was a means to get your work on display for the school." *Tad must have had these thoughts bottled up for a while*, I thought. *And now that he's started, he intends to finish.* "Sometimes we'd be together, and I'd think we were really having a great time. Then I'd ask you to get a soda or go out for supplies, and you'd invite Elaine or one of your friends to join us." Tad's chin jutted forward, and his eyes looked defensive. "So, what's the story tonight, Donna? Is it 'Let's cheer up Tad because he's nervous before the election,' or what?"

"Oh, Tad, no," I said, overwhelmed that he cared so much. "Tonight was terrific." I smiled shyly. "Listen, Tad. I was aware of you long before you ever met me." The wariness was

118

still in his eyes. I was so anxious to convince him that I was sincere that I blurted out what I'd vowed I'd never reveal to anyone, especially Tad. I told him that he'd been the model for my Roman god art project earlier that semester.

He laughed, and I suddenly felt his strong arm around my shoulder. "I'd like to see it some time," he said softly and then his lips brushed across mine in an almost-kiss. I got out of Tad's car feeling so light-headed that I practically floated to the front door.

A half hour later I sat in bed, reliving each minute of the evening we'd spent together. I still couldn't believe what had happened. Imagine, a guy like Tad Gordon feeling so insecure and nervous about *me*! I didn't think I'd ever get to sleep. What was the point? I was already living the best dream I could possibly imagine.

The next morning I called Sandy, eager to talk to her about my date. I told her it had been wonderful, but I didn't reveal every detail. Some things between Tad and me would have to stay private. "I'm *soooo* happy that everything worked out so well," Sandy said. "Did he ask you to the Victory Dance?"

I'd forgotten all about it. "Well, no, not yet," I said with my newfound confidence. "But I really think he will." I thought that if he hadn't said anything about it by Monday, I might hint around, just to let him know that I did want to be with him, no matter who won.

During the campaign meeting at my house Sunday night, Tad offered to pick up some more soda and munchies at a convenience store a few miles away. Winking at me, he said, "Don't work too hard while I'm gone, guys. Hey, Donna, why don't you walk me out to the car?"

When I returned to the family room, I heard Sandy saying to Ellen, Elaine, and a couple of the other kids who were painting, "Well, they did go out together Saturday night, and they really like each other." I groaned inwardly, hoping Sandy wouldn't say anything more.

The rest of the evening passed fairly uneventfully. Everyone agreed that it was fun to have a reason to get together so often. In a way it would be sad when the campaign ended.

Before we knew it, it had gotten very late, and almost everyone, including Tad, had gone home. I gathered up some brushes and went to wash them out in the kitchen sink. When Elaine followed, offering to help, I noticed that her beautiful almond eyes looked troubled. She handed me the brushes to rinse one at a time, and said, "You know, Donna, I'd really hate to see you get hurt, so I hope you won't mind my being a little brutal. I've known Tad a long time. Believe me, I'm only saying this now so you won't be upset later."

I put the brushes down on the counter. "What is it, Elaine?"

She sighed, studying the heavy gold bracelet on her wrist. "Well, Tad is what he is. Charming. Fun. But in spite of what he says now, he likes your art, not you. And when the campaign is over, I'm afraid your relationship will be, too."

I could feel tears forming in my eyes. "That's not true," I said defensively. "You don't know anything about Tad and me."

"Oh, Donna." There was an edge of scorn in Elaine's voice. "Don't be so naive. The fact is, Tad may have been interested in you for the past couple of weeks, but you're almost history. I'll prove it to you, OK? If Tad really were interested in you, he'd have asked you to the Victory Dance. He hasn't, has he?"

"Well—" I began.

"See." Elaine's eyes blazed in triumph. "And he won't because he's going to the dance with Christy."

"But, that's impossible. Look what she did to him."

Elaine shrugged. "The election is almost over. Whoever wins, wins. Tad and Christy will never have to run against each other again. Maybe when the election is out of the way, they'll decide there are things they still like about each other. They used to be quite a couple, believe me." My mouth fell open, as an awful picture of Tad kissing Christy materialized in my mind. "Hey, I'm only trying to help," Elaine said, walking out of the kitchen.

Tears stung my cheeks, and I tried to wipe them away quickly. I couldn't let anyone see me crying like that. Someone called from the other room, asking me where I wanted him to put a poster while it dried. I didn't answer right away, but I knew I'd have to go back and face the last couple of kids sooner or later. Splashing cold water on my face at the sink, I forced myself to go into the family room and act as if nothing had happened. Fortunately, they were getting ready to leave, and I only had to carry on my little charade for a few minutes. I didn't say another word to Elaine, and she left without even saying goodbye.

Chapter Eleven

All that night I had terrible nightmares, and I tossed and turned in my bed. After waking up at six, I gave up trying to go back to sleep. Over and over in my mind, I attempted to make sense of the whole situation with Tad. He didn't have to take me out. I'd have worked on his campaign, anyway. Besides, even if Tad did ask me out, he didn't have to say all the things he had. We could have gone out, had some laughs, and that would have been the end of it. I hadn't pushed Tad to say I mattered to him. He'd been the one to bring the whole thing up, and unless he was the world's best actor, he *did* seem to care about me.

I felt better after reasoning through the whole thing, but why would Elaine have gone out of her way to be spiteful? I'd certainly never done anything to her. Still, there'd been something about the girl that I hadn't liked or trusted right from the beginning. That first night at Tad's house, she'd walked in with her hand possessively on his arm. Could Elaine be jealous of me? I shook my head. That was just too crazy to believe. A popular, pretty senior intimidated by me? But maybe, just maybe, if she liked Tad enough and she thought Tad liked me, well . . .

I got out of bed and started to get ready for school. Whom should I believe? Either Elaine was a conniving witch, or Tad was a total creep. Of the two I preferred to think that Elaine was a witch. But what if she'd only been trying to keep me from making a fool of myself? Maybe I was so crazy about Tad that I wasn't seeing the truth. I yanked the brush through my hair. *Well, Donna, there's one way to find out,* I told myself. *Pretend nothing has happened, and tell Tad that you'd like to go to the Victory Dance with him.* There was no doubt I'd find out that way whether or not Elaine was telling the truth.

My classes that morning were a total waste of time. I didn't hear a word my teachers said. I was so preoccupied that when Sandy mentioned at lunch that she thought that day's cartoon was the best of all, I realized that I hadn't even gone by the library to see it.

124

"Sandy," I said, turning my thoughts back to Tad and Christy, "are there any traditions about the Victory Dance that I might not be aware of?"

"Like what?" she asked, looking at me strangely.

I blushed. "Oh, I don't know. Like whether the two candidates have to go together or anything?"

Sandy laughed, "Are you kidding? A few years ago, both candidates were guys, and the year before that, there were two girls." Then her face grew serious. "Oh, I get it. Tad still hasn't said anything about the dance, huh?"

I shook my head and opened my yogurt. I wasn't all that hungry. Just then Tad showed up at our table. My heart leaped in spite of my determination to stay calm.

Tad pulled up a chair next to mine and sat down. "Hi, Donna. Sorry I had to leave early last night. But wait until you see the skit we wrote for the assembly on Thursday! We're going to have our first rehearsal at tomorrow night's sign-painting party." He went on as if nothing in the world had changed between us since Saturday night.

More than anything, I wanted to blurt out my question about whether he was taking Christy to the Victory Dance. With all those people around, though, it just wasn't the time or place.

Somehow, for the next two days, it never seemed to be the right time or place. Twice Tad had referred to me as his girlfriend, which was a positive sign, but time was running out. The skits were the next day, voting was Friday, and the Victory Dance was Friday night—just two days away, and Tad still hadn't mentioned it to me. The last cartoon had gone up on the library wall, and our Tad the Terrific story would be finished in the skit at Thursday's assembly. Even though he'd given me no real reason to doubt him, I almost believed that when the last poster came down, Tad would disappear from my life.

As I walked toward my last-period class, Tad's long legs fell in step with mine. "Well, I guess you're about to retire from the sign-making business, huh? How about if we go out after school and celebrate?"

Relief flooded my body. I wasn't getting dumped after all! Now would be the perfect time to straighten out the Victory Dance problem. I was so glad I hadn't gone and done anything stupid. Elaine was either greatly misinformed or really mean. I told Tad I'd meet him after school.

When things started going right, they really went well. I walked into my last class—French—to find a bonus question on the board. Bonus questions were never directly related to what we were studying at the time, but if we knew the answer, we could earn ten extra-credit points. Usually, I had no idea what the answers were, but the other night I'd read the wrong assignment—the pages about the question on the board. At the time I'd been really mad at myself for miscopying the page numbers. But it was certainly paying off, though. My pen flew across the paper. Maybe things would work out that well with Tad.

It was a beautiful day, and I suggested that we leave the car in the parking lot and walk to Swensen's. Slipping his hand into mine, Tad agreed, and we started off. Out of the corner of my eye, I saw Elaine standing next to her car, frowning at us. I decided to forget all about her.

By the time we got to Swensen's, the initial after-school rush was over, so we were waited on immediately. We each chose double-dip chocolate ice-cream cones and left the store to begin walking back to school, hand in hand. "This is really nice," Tad said. "I think it's just what I needed. I'd been getting pretty uptight all day about tomorrow's skit. I wish

127

you'd designed our costumes. I know they'd look a lot better than the ones we've scraped together."

I asked him if he had any idea what Christy was going to do for her speech, but he didn't know. It seemed to me that he shifted the conversation away from her very quickly, but then it could have been my own paranoia.

At the edge of the school grounds we stopped, and I squeezed Tad's hand and smiled. "You've done the best you possibly could," I assured him. "That's all that counts. I hope you win, but I'll care about you just as much if you don't. I'm looking forward to the Victory Dance, whether you're the new student-body president or not."

There! I'd said it. After all my careful planning, the words had suddenly popped out. A crazy mixture of hope and fear filled my heart as I turned toward Tad to hear his response.

"Donna," Tad began, hesitating as if he didn't know what to say. "I can't take you to the Victory Dance."

"Why not?" My words came out in a half-accusing whisper. "Are you taking Christy?"

"Donna . . ."

Had Elaine been right after all? "Are you taking Christy?" I repeated.

Tad looked very uncomfortable. "Well, yes, but—"

I didn't want to hear the rest of his words. Tearing my hand from his, I ran into the school to the safety of the girls' bathroom. Out of breath and completely flushed, I finally released the big sobs that had been wracking me.

I guess I must have sat crying on the bathroom floor for at least half an hour. After a while no more tears would come. Slowly I stood up, wondering how I'd even have the strength to get home.

Tad was nowhere to be seen when I emerged from the building. I tried to sort things out as I walked, but nothing was clear except that Elaine had been right. Maybe she'd been a little blunt in the way she'd delivered her news, but at least she'd really been a friend who was trying to keep me from getting hurt. And then, there was Tad. All false charm and fake vulnerability, and I'd fallen for every bit of it. What had been the point of his toying with me? Had he just been building up his ego, or had he really wanted to hurt me for some reason? Maybe that was how guys that cute and that popular got their kicks.

If only I'd stuck to my original plan not to get involved.

Chapter Twelve

The seven blocks to my house seemed like seventeen miles. Even getting up the walk to the front door took a lot of effort. I just wanted to get to my room, go to sleep, and forget the whole day. Maybe I could even erase the last couple of weeks from my mind.

My mom heard me unlock the front door. "Donna, is that you?" she called. I had heard her banging away on the typewriter. She worked at home.

"Yes," I called back. "I'm going to lie down. I've had an exhausting day."

My mother came out of her office. "Well, I've got—" She stopped in midsentence. "Donna, you look terrible! Are you getting sick?"

"No, Mom, I'm OK," I said, wishing she'd leave me alone.

"Well, you don't look it," she replied, tapping her foot. "Tad came by, honey. He waited for you a few minutes, and when you didn't come home, he asked you to call him." She looked at me closely. "Did you two have a fight or something?"

"No, it wasn't really a fight. More of a mis-understanding." I bit my lip to keep the tears from starting again. "Right now, Mom, I don't even want to talk about it." My mother was really good about things like that, and she never pushed too much. If I ever got my feel-ings sorted out, maybe I'd be able to explain to her what had happened between Tad and me.

Entering my room, I dropped my backpack by the door and flopped onto my bed. I put a hand across my eyes to shut out the light, but my brain wouldn't stop racing. I was hurt, angry, and totally humiliated. Tad must have gotten quite a kick out of my confession about using him for the model of my Roman god.

The phone rang, but I had no intention of getting up to answer it. My mother knocked hesitantly on my door. "Honey, Tad's on the phone. I think you might as well talk to him and get things straightened out."

"Not yet, Mom," I pleaded. "Have him call back, OK? I have to decide what I want to say."

"All right, Donna," she said disapprovingly. "This once I will, but your problems won't just go away, you know. You have to work at solving them."

I turned my face to the wall.

For the rest of the evening, I plotted little speeches to give Tad when he called back. I shouldn't have wasted my time. By ten o'clock I realized that Tad wasn't going to call me again. While I'd been pacing my room and crying, he'd probably been off partying with a bunch of his friends or practicing his part for the skit.

As I left for school the next morning, I felt like a limp rag. There was an air of excitement in the hallways as people talked about the upcoming assembly, but I wasn't a part of it. "This is the most intense campaign I've ever seen at Washington," I overheard one teacher telling another as we filed into the auditorium. "I wonder what they'll come up with for their presentations."

I took a seat in the back of the auditorium. I could see that a lot of the kids who'd worked on Tad's campaign were sitting together. I could always say later that I couldn't find them. Right then, I had so many mixed feelings that I figured it would probably be better for me to sit alone. It was strange simply being a part of the background after having been so intensely involved in Tad's campaign. Part of me wanted him to come out in that ridiculous Tad the Terrific cape and fall flat on his face. *I hope Christy wins!* I thought meanly. *It would serve him right.*

The image of Tad's face as he'd talked about his chances for the election filled my mind. He wanted to win so badly, and I had to admit it had been fun to work on the campaign. Lots of kids knew me who hadn't known me before, and Mrs. Gibbons had raved about my cartoons. She had said they'd helped me loosen up, just as she'd hoped they would. Maybe in spite of everything that had happened, I did still want Tad to win. But now I only knew that, instead of being one of the group who was cheering wildly when Tad came onstage, I was sitting in the back row feeling betrayed and humiliated.

The skit was a great success. The kids in it managed to bring the cartoon to life perfectly, and Tad was a real ham. He played Tad the Terrific to the hilt. Why should I have been so surprised? He'd certainly been a good actor around me. By the end of the skit, the crowd was clapping and whistling and calling for more.

It would be interesting to see how Christy would try to top Tad's skit. I almost felt sorry for her because I didn't think there was any way she could do it. In fact, if I'd had to lay odds, I'd have said without even seeing Christy's skit that Tad had won the election. Mr. Lunder was having a hard time even getting all the students calmed down. *I wouldn't want to be in Christy's shoes right now,* I told myself. Then I thought of the dance the following night. Christy could take care of herself.

Finally the auditorium was quiet, and Christy walked out onstage. She was beautiful. Her hair looked like spun gold under the lights, and she wore an elegant ivory dress. She was very much alone on stage. Taking the microphone from its stand, she began to talk, making the audience feel as if she were speaking to each one of them as her best friend.

"Tomorrow you are going to elect someone to run this school for the last semester," Christy began. "For you seniors, it will be your last semester of high school. It will also be the final weeks of our being together as a group before we go our separate ways. Many of us may never see one another again. We deserve to have our last few weeks made really special. Juniors, sophomores, and freshmen, you deserve no less than to have some new and very special traditions created for you, memories that will live on long after you leave Washington."

Christy stopped speaking, and there wasn't a single sound in the auditorium. Even though she wasn't holding any note cards, her speech didn't sound memorized. It sounded as if she were having a heart-to-heart talk with a friend. "Naturally, anyone who runs for office wants to win," she went on. "And I, too, would like a victory. But I don't think you should vote for me unless you like the ideas I'm proposing." Christy then began to describe some really interesting projects she'd planned for the new semester. I especially liked her suggestions about the prom. "If you agree with what you've heard, if you feel that my ideas will help make Washington a better place, then I ask you to vote for me."

The crowd began to clap, first softly and then louder and louder. Christy had taken the exact opposite approach from Tad. She couldn't have topped his humor. She hadn't even tried. Tad had come off as being clever and funny; Christy seemed thoughtful and thorough. Her ideas might even carry the election. The applause finally died down, and Christy still stood alone on the stage. Then, in his ridiculous Tad the Terrific costume, Tad joined her. He walked over, shook her hand, and kissed her on the cheek. The crowd went absolutely wild.

I clenched my teeth in anger. Tad sure hadn't wasted any time! Blindly, I fought my way out of the auditorium and stormed to my locker. I couldn't wait to get out of that dumb school that day, and I still had to go to one more class. Why didn't they have assemblies last thing in the afternoon? Then at least I could go home and be alone in my misery.

When I got to class, everyone was talking about the presentations. Some kids were arguing that Tad's skit was the funniest thing they'd ever seen, and how could anyone vote against Tad the Terrific? Others contended that Tad's skit was ridiculous and that Christy's image was much more impressive. One girl pointed out, "How can we ever get the administration to take us seriously if we elect some guy who runs around in a cape? Our prom plans won't have a chance."

The teacher got tired of trying to lecture over the ongoing whispers. He finally threw up his hands and gave in. "I'll tell you one thing," he said. "I've never seen students get so excited over a school campaign." Stroking his chin, he added, "And I'm not sure that's such a good idea. The principal told us there were three fistfights this week, all started over who should win the election."

Finally the bell rang. I didn't want to hear another word about the whole campaign as long as I lived. I tore out the door, without even stopping at my locker. Suddenly a tall figure blocked my path. Tad. He smiled and put his hand on my shoulder.

There was no escaping this. I vowed to myself that I wouldn't let him see how much he'd hurt me. "Hello, Tad," I said, gritting my teeth. "Your skit went really well."

Smiling, he patted my head as if I were some little puppy dog. "Oh, Donna, I'm so glad you're not mad at me anymore. I never would have guessed that you had such a temper."

My eyes were burning, but I tried to keep my voice calm. "I was upset, Tad. I still am. You never said a word to me about the Victory Dance."

"Look, Donna, I don't blame you for being upset. I guess I should have told you about everything sooner, but I just didn't think of it. Can't you just forgive me, and we'll start over again now? We'll have plenty of time together after the election."

Just then, my temper exploded. "Tad, you sound just like a politician trying to placate one last voter. Well, forget it!"

Tad's smile vanished. "Oh, come on. That's a low blow. Why can't you just trust me when I say that everything will work out? I'm nervous enough about this election, and I really don't need this from you. I could use a little support right now, Donna. I'm really sorry if you thought I was taking you to the Victory

Dance, but I can't. It's only one night, and it's not like I made a date with you and then stood you up, either. I'm really sorry if I hurt your feelings. I had no idea you'd get so upset." His voice trailed away, and he looked sincerely miserable.

I sucked in my breath. I could read between the lines. He wanted me to be a good little girl and adore him from afar. I should be glad for the date I'd had with him. I was sure that's what he had meant. Maybe I'd never really had a chance with Tad at all, and I'd already made enough of a fool of myself by letting him think I cared so much. At least I could try to salvage what was left of my pride.

"Don't worry about it, Tad," I snapped, staring right into those blue, blue eyes of his. "It's really no big deal. Christy was the first choice for both of us. I only came to work on your campaign as a last resort. I needed a higher grade in art, and working on a school project for the election was the only way Mrs. Gibbons would raise my grade. I asked Christy first, and she turned me down. So, you see, there are no hurt feelings. You got good campaign art, and I got a better grade. We should both be very happy."

Tad looked stunned. "You really went to Christy first?"

"That's right," I answered. I could see Tad kissing Christy again in my mind. "And, if you don't believe me, you can always ask her about it at the dance tomorrow night." I stuck out my hand. "Good luck, Tad. I'll see you around."

Tad ignored my thrust-out hand and stormed past me. He muttered something to himself about having been warned, that he should have listened, but I really didn't hear all of what he said.

Shaking, I ran all the way home and crawled into bed, telling my mother I was sick. I wasn't really lying, because I felt terrible. I slept through what was left of the day, and before I knew it, it was time for school the next morning.

Ironically, the junior class voted during art. For a long time, I stared at my ballot. *I'll show him.* I thought. *I'll vote for Christy.* But when it came right down to it, I just couldn't check off her name. It was my own fault I'd fallen for Tad. He'd only promised me that I could run his election art, and I'd done exactly that. He'd never said I could be his girlfriend. The vision of Tad's forlorn face when he'd told me how badly he wanted to win flashed in my mind. I marked my ballot for Tad Gordon.

Mrs. Gibbons called me up to her desk at the end of the class. "Donna," she said. "I don't know if your candidate will win, but I wanted to tell you that your cartoons were some of the cleverest I've ever seen. I thought that today would be an appropriate time to give you your corrected report card. Congratulations. You've more than earned your A."

I tried to muster some real enthusiasm as I thanked Mrs. Gibbons. I'd almost forgotten how much I'd wanted—needed—that grade.

As I walked out of class, I had to fight back tears. How ironic. A few weeks ago, that A would have made me so happy. Now it wasn't enough. Even the Art Institute of America seemed very far away.

Somehow I got through the day. There was another fight at lunch and a rumor going around that kids were trying to forge ballots. I didn't pay attention to any of it.

Sandy kept telling me that I just *had* to go to the Victory Dance. "Don't you want to be there to at least find out who wins?" she insisted. "You spent every waking minute on this campaign for the last few weeks. Look, Donna, something's wrong. I know it. I'm *sure* that Tad likes you for real."

After she'd started up again for the tenth time, I lost patience. "Oh, Sandy, just leave me alone, OK? Please. I want to be my myself tonight. I'm not going to the dance, and I'm forgetting all about Tad. Did you see him kiss Christy in the assembly yesterday? You told me to ignore Elaine's warning about Tad, but she was right. You wanted it all to work out, and I appreciate that, but it didn't. It's over."

Everyone was talking about the Victory Dance. Rumors had been flying all afternoon, but no one could predict for sure who had won the election. There was going to be a terrific turnout for the dance.

During last period, the girl in front of me turned to the girl next to her and said, "Guess what! I just heard that Christy is Tad's date for the dance! Can you believe it, after the way they've practically been at each other's throats?"

The boy in back of me chimed in. "Hey, haven't you two ever heard of kissing and making up? With the right girl, that can be a pretty good reason to fight!" He smirked. "Tad's no fool. What guy would pass up a chance to kiss Christy?"

I bit my lip so hard that it almost bled, and the minutes on the clock ticked slowly, slowly away.

Chapter Thirteen

School was finally out for the weekend. On Monday there'd be a whole new set of things for people to gossip about. Everyone would know who had won the election, and the cartoons that had made me popular would be well on their way to being forgotten.

. Feeling thoroughly sorry for myself, I trudged home alone. At dinner that night my mom and dad suggested that I go to the movies with them, but I said I was too tired. "We could all stay home and play Monopoly," my mother suggested in a cheery voice.

"Mom, I'm OK. Really, I am." I forced a smile. "You and Dad go ahead. I'm going to take a hot bath and relax."

After my parents left, I sat in my room,

142

clutching my pillow and trying not to watch the clock. I kept wondering if Christy and Tad were dancing all the slow dances, and how much longer it would be until the results of the election were announced. Miserably, my head reminded my heart how much I'd wanted to be the girl in Tad's arms that night.

I'd just settled into a hot bubble bath, when the phone rang. It had to be Tad! I knew it! He'd won, and he was calling to say that he wanted me with him. My heart pounding, I grabbed a towel and ran to the phone. It was only nine-thirty. I could be dressed in no time, and we could still spend the rest of the evening together. "Don't stop ringing, phone, I'm coming!" I shouted happily. Grabbing the receiver moments later, I practically yelled, "Hello!"

"I was beginning to think you weren't home."

"Oh, hi, Sandy." I hoped she wouldn't hear the disappointment in my voice.

"Tad won! Tad won!" she cried joyfully. "But that's not why I'm calling. I only have a minute because I told Andy I'd be right back. Listen up, and listen good. I just went into the girls' bathroom, and you'll never *believe* what I heard! Christy came in to comb her hair with one of her friends, and she didn't know that I was there. I mean, I was in one of the stalls. Her friend asked something about how it was being with Tad again, and Christy said it was OK but they were just friends. So here's the good part. Are you ready? Christy said that Mr. Lunder had asked them to go to the dance together because the campaign had been really tense, and he didn't want any more trouble." Sandy took a minute to catch her breath. "So, you see," she said triumphantly, "Tad *had* to take her. And that's not all. Christy said she could hardly wait for the dance to be over because this new college guy she likes is taking her out afterward. Then the friend laughed and said that maybe Tad would turn to Elaine, now that Christy was out of the picture. Christy said that'd be great, because Elaine has had a crush on Tad forever." Sandy's voice was practically squeaking with excitement. "Donna, did you hear me? You were set up! Tad doesn't want Christy, and he doesn't want Elaine! Listen, we're having a party at Tad's after the dance breaks up. I'll have Andy stop by for you on our way. You can come and apologize to Tad, and everything will be great! I've go to go, OK? I'll see you at about ten-thirty!"

The line went dead. Standing there in my

towel, dripping all over the carpet, I was too dumbfounded to move. I needed time to sort this whole thing out. Elaine had made sure I'd know that Tad was taking Christy to the dance, but she hadn't told me the reason. Why not? Because if I wasn't there, she could have Tad all to herself.

I thought of the terrible way I'd treated Tad. I hadn't even given him a chance to explain why he was taking Christy to the dance. I remembered with shame how I'd acted the last time I'd spoken to him. He probably never wanted to see me again.

More than anything in the world, I wanted to go to Tad's party and tell him that I was sorry and that I did care. I ran back to my room and began to pull clothes out of my closet. Sandy and Andy would be there before I knew it.

I pulled on a pair of black jeans and a fuzzy white sweater. Looking in the mirror, I tried to practice what I would say. "Hi, Tad," I greeted my reflection. "I bet you're surprised to see me." That sounded terrible. I tried again. "Hi, Tad. Congratulations." That was better, but then what would I say? I couldn't very well explain everything in front of a roomful of people. It wouldn't work to go barging in and ask Tad to leave everyone to come outside and talk, either.

I sighed. A girl like Christy might be able to pull something like that off, but not me. What could I do? Suddenly, an idea hit me. I took out my sketch pad and began a cartoon. I didn't have much time, but I knew just what I wanted to draw. I drew myself, red-faced and wearing a big dunce cap on my head. "I'm really sorry," I wrote at the top of the page. In the next frame I wore a big valentine-type heart on my dress that said "Tad is terrific." In the cartoon balloon above my head I printed "I'm so glad you won." Then I drew Tad in his full costume and had him saying, "Because I'm a superhero, I forgive you." In the last box, I had my two cartoon figures gazing into each other's eyes, with a big heart around the two of them. It was corny, but the caricatures of both of us were funny. It was the only way I could express to Tad the way I was feeling. Maybe the art that had brought us together in the first place would do its magic again.

Sandy rang the doorbell about five minutes after I'd finished coloring the last panel. I stuck the whole thing into a big envelope and ran to the door.

"You don't even have your shoes on!" Sandy wailed, "And your hair's still wet. Donna, what's . . ."

"Sandy, you're the best friend in the whole world, but I just can't go over there tonight. Give this to Tad for me, and cross your fingers that everything works out, OK?"

"But—" A car horn honked insistently. Sandy looked torn. "I've got to go," she said, glancing back. "But I sure hope whatever this is works."

I closed the door softly. *Me, too,* I thought.

After Sandy had left, I nervously paced back and forth around the house. "Let's see," I said aloud, staring at the clock. "It shouldn't take them more than five minutes to get to Tad's from here. Then it'll take Sandy another few minutes to find him. It might take some more time before Tad can get away from the crowd and find a quiet spot to call. . . ." It was ten-twenty. That meant I should definitely hear from Tad by eleven. I sat down to wait. The clock seemed frozen at ten-twenty. I just couldn't stand it. I had to find some way to make the minutes pass until the phone rang. I jumped up to turn on the TV in the family room, but I couldn't focus on the screen.

Finally I decided to go ahead and finish dressing and doing my hair and makeup. I doubted that Tad would leave everyone at the party and come over, but it was a possibility. Besides, I'd been wrong about predicting everything else. Maybe he was already on his way.

With that exciting thought, I ran back to my room to get ready. In a way it seemed ludicrous to be getting dressed at the time I was usually getting ready for bed, but if Tad was going to show up, the least I could do was look my best.

By eleven I looked as good as I ever would, but the phone hadn't rung at all. I tried to tell myself that it might have taken Sandy awhile to get the picture to Tad, but I was rapidly losing hope. Then I heard a car pulling up the driveway. My heart went into positive overdrive. I couldn't believe it! Tad was actually here! He'd left his own party to come get me. My eyes welled with tears, and I dabbed them away so as not to smear my makeup. Smiling and radiant, I hurried to the front door.

To my surprise, it opened just as I got downstairs. "Mom, Dad," I said, feeling sick, "it's you."

"Right," replied my dad. "We live here, remember? How come you're so dressed up?"

I blushed self-consciously. "Oh, it's a long story. I, uh, thought Tad might drop by tonight."

"Well, if you ask me, he certainly should

have," my father said. "Not only did you work yourself to death on his campaign, but you look beautiful."

"Thanks, Dad," I said, touched. "But you don't quite know the whole story." I bit my lip. "I was pretty dumb. I guess I know that now, and I found it out too late." I sighed deeply and turned back toward the stairs. "I'm going to bed. See you in the morning."

The next morning when I woke up, I desperately wanted to talk to Sandy. I even felt a little embarrassed about that. I mean, what if Sandy had given him the picture, and he'd opened it in front of everyone? Maybe he'd made a joke about it. I told myself that it'd be better to let the whole thing go. Even if Sandy called, I wasn't going to bring up the party.

When the phone rang, however, my resolve lasted less than two minutes. Sandy talked about the party nonstop and told me over and over how many times she and Andy had danced. I was happy for her, but I couldn't stand waiting to hear about Tad's reaction to my card.

"So," I attempted casually, "did you give Tad my envelope?"

"Yeah, I did." Sandy paused. "I made sure I found him right after we got there. I almost waited because Elaine was pretty much hanging all over him, but I thought it might be important for him to get it right away." She sighed.

"Go on," I urged. "Tell me what happened. I can take it."

"Well, I told him it was from you, but he put it down on the table. So I said, 'Aren't you going to open it, Tad?' And Elaine laughed and said the campaign was all over, and the guy deserved a break." Sandy's voice sounded discouraged. "Then someone put on a good song, and everyone started dancing. Later, Donna, when I looked, the envelope wasn't on the table anymore. I'll bet Elaine threw it away. Are you even going to tell me what was in it?"

"It doesn't matter, Sandy. It was just a cartoon. Listen, I want to thank you for everything, but I don't really feel like talking right now."

Sandy said she understood, and we hung up. I sat in my room, staring at my corkboard art wall and feeling perfectly miserable. Finally I took my sketch book and went out to sit under a big tree in the backyard. The ground was cold, hard, and uncomfortable. It fit right in with my mood, and I drew somber pictures in shades of gray and black.

Intent on my work, I didn't even glance up when I heard footsteps behind me. Suddenly a deep male voice I knew well said, "Got any time to spend with a beginning artist?"

"Tad!" I gasped. "What are *you* doing here?" I bit my tongue. That hadn't been what I'd wanted to say at all.

His piercing blue eyes glared at me like cold lasers. "Donna, I'm here because I thought you wanted me to come. I figured we needed to talk. Maybe I was wrong on both counts." There was a guarded edge to his voice, and I knew that if I blew this chance, I'd never get another.

"Tad." My voice sounded shaky and a little too formal. "I'm so glad you're here. Congratulations on winning the election. I'm really happy for you."

"Thanks," he replied. "Without your cartoons, I might not have won."

There was an uneasy silence between us, as if we were two strangers going through some polite thank-you ritual. I thought of all the fun times we'd had working on the campaign and being together, and my heart grew heavy. Maybe we could never recapture those feelings. I wanted to blurt out that I thought he was the greatest guy I'd ever met, but I couldn't get the words past my throat. I was too embarrassed.

"I, uh, I'm sorry that I didn't go to the dance last night or to your party." I took a deep breath. "What I said about only wanting to work on your campaign for an art grade wasn't true. It was one of the best times of my life. And I couldn't stop thinking about you all last night."

Tad's toe scraped the dirt. "Donna, I had to take Christy to that dance. Mr. Lunder was concerned that there might be some fights when the election results were announced. He practically begged Christy and me to go together so we could show everyone that there were no hard feelings. I guess I should have told you, but I didn't think it was that big a deal. Really, Christy doesn't mean anything to me anymore. Mr. Lunder has helped the student council out lots of times, and we felt kind of obligated to him. I honestly didn't want to hurt you, but I was pretty steamed when you wouldn't even give me a chance to explain."

I couldn't look at Tad at all. It didn't seem like the right time to tell him about Elaine. "I guess," I said, barely whispering, "I was afraid of losing you."

"Really?" Tad laughed, and I felt myself being pulled to my feet.

"Tad—" I began. Then his arms wrapped around me, and I felt the delicious sensation of his lips on mine.

When we finally parted, Tad kept one arm protectively around my shoulders. "You know,

Donna," he said tenderly, "I think I've wanted to do that ever since the first day I met you."

Resting my head against his shoulder, I said dreamily, "I definitely think you should have."

"Well, geez, Donna, you sure don't give a guy much encouragement. Every time I arranged for us to be alone together, you'd include Elaine or Sandy or somebody."

My eyes were shining. "Tad, I was just scared. I guess I couldn't really believe that a guy like you would want to be with a girl like me."

"Yeah?" he asked teasingly as he held me tighter. "And exactly what is wrong with a girl like you?"

"Well, I'm not gorgeous or popular like Elaine and Christy. I mean, when you didn't respond to my cartoon last night, well, I figured—"

Tad kissed me again softly. When he drew away he said, "Donna, I really didn't know what was in that envelope Sandy gave me, but I was feeling pretty hurt and betrayed about what you'd said about working on my campaign. I knew that whatever you'd sent me, I wanted to be alone when I opened it, because you're *not* like Christy or Elaine." His voice got husky, and he added, "If you were, you wouldn't matter so much to me." Tad suddenly looked embarrassed and tried to lighten the mood. "Now, about this art lesson I came for," he said. "Let me show you my unique style."

We sat down under the tree together. It no longer seemed like a cold, uncomfortable spot, but warm and cozy. Picking up one of my pencils, Tad drew two stick figures and labeled them *Donna* and *Tad*. Around them he drew a large, rather lopsided heart. "Well, what do you think?" he asked, grinning.

"I think it shows absolutely zero artistic ability," I replied. Tad looked crushed. Gazing into his deep blue eyes, I added, "And it's the most beautiful picture I've ever seen."

Tad drew me into his arms again. "I guess I'll need to spend a long time working with a particular artist."

"Oh yes," I agreed happily. "A *very* long time."